Greek Mythology

KATERINA SERVI
Archaeologist

EKDOTIKE ATHENON S.A.
Athens 2002

Publisher: A. Christopoulos
Co-ordinator of the publication: Ioannis C. Bastias

Editor: Myrto Stavropoulou
Translation: Cox & Solman, Athens
Art editing: Irini Kalogera
Illustrations: Evi Atzemi
Cover design: Angela Simou
Map: Tonia Kotsoni
Colour reproduction, printing and binding:
Ekdotike Hellados SA, 8 Philadelpheias St, Athens

ISBN 960-213-373-2

Contents

Prefix

At a time when man was still in the initial stage of his civilisation and his thought had not yet consciously come to serve objective truth, the resort to myth was the only way to supply an answer to the questions which exercised him, to interpret natural phenomena, and to preserve what he himself had seen, experienced and imagined and thought should not be forgotten. Particularly in the case of those myths which deal with human history, it is very likely that there is some kernel of actual history embedded in them, just as it is not impossible that some of the heroes of whom they tell were real people, whether they bore the names ascribed to them or others. Naturally, the tracing of the actual circumstances which gave rise to the creation of each myth is not possible, since the traditions in question have been enriched with a host of poetical features, but also because the people and the bard who forged the myth did not regard themselves as under any obligation to remain faithful to historical truth.

Greek myth owes its immortality - often in many varied versions - to the fact that it was cultivated for at least fourteen centuries in the places where it was born by a host of epic, lyric and dramatic poets, who wished to make of it a vehicle for the ideals of the Greek world. Many typical features of the Greek spirit are imprinted on the myth - a tendency towards competition, the affirmation of life, the worship of beauty, and the interest of the Greeks in man as man, leading to the creation of an idealised picture of him, which served to promote rules of life of general authority.

A great many peoples from one end of the earth to the other have a mythology of gods and heroes. It is, however, only ancient Greek mythology which, thanks to its quality, has transcended every geographical and chronological frontier and has become a possession of the human spirit as a whole.

It has been our wish in this volume to provide a Mythology which is not addressed only to specialists - though without losing its scholarly character - but which will be accessible to a wide range of the public; a Mythology which will be read with pleasure by children and adults, by scholars and intellectuals, but also by ordinary people who, without any interest in the specialist questions of academic research, wish to be entertained by discovering what stories the ancient Greeks told about their gods and heroes and to enjoy in a straightforward manner the beauty of the ancient myths.

COSMOGONY
Cosmogony
COSMOGONY

COSMOGONY

*I*n the beginning ... was the myth'. In prehistoric times, man found himself at a loss before the magnitude of the universe, unable to comprehend the world and interpret natural phenomena by the power of reasoning. The vital need to provide answers to the questions which concerned him, to give a shape to all these unseen powers which caused him astonishment, perplexity and fear, led him to devise a mythological account of the origin of the world - his own version of cosmogony.

There are many ancient Greek myths which deal with the beginning of creation. The state of affairs before the creation, which most myth-makers imagined as without order, dark, cold, and without stable outlines, was succeeded by the appearance of certain self-generated entities such as Chaos or Tartarus, Aer or Oceanus, Night or Erebus. These gave life to the first gods, who, with the passage of time, were replaced by other, younger, ones. The conflict between the older and the younger divinities, which resulted in the triumph of the younger generation, reflects the concept of the subjugation of the primordial, less perfect and more savage powers to the will of others, more perfect and tamed.

A very important part of the account of the cosmogony is, naturally enough, the creation of the human race. Here too the imagination of the ancient Greeks did not confine itself to one version only. For some, men were

Selene (the Moon) rises from the sea. (Interior of an Attic red-figure kylix, by the Brygus Painter, c. 485 BC).

Helios (the Sun) and Eos (Dawn), children of the Titan Hyperion, are shown in the firmament. On the left, Night, and on the right Dawn, in their chariots, are journeying. Between them the radiant Sun rises in his four-horse chariot. (White lekythos, 5th century BC).

Helios (the Sun), bottom left, is driving his chariot, which climbs steeply. Further to the right can still be seen a part of the horse of Selene (the Moon); she herself has already disappeared. To the right, winged Night with her chariot is also disappearing. (Red-figure lid of a box - pyxis - 5th century BC).

made by the gods, for others, by the Titan Prometheus. Other myths, derived from the traditions of different localities, speak of men coming from the earth itself or of mortals being born from the mating of deities.

It is particularly interesting to compare Greek creation myths with those of other nations. In some instances research has brought to light close connections between Greek and non-Greek cosmogonies. The story of Cronus, as related by Hesiod, shows striking similarities with the Kumarbi epic, discovered on the tablets of the Hittite state archive, which date from the 14th - 13th century BC. The narration of Hesiod seems to have been modelled on an earlier Hittite text, while Cronus is to be identified, even etymologically, with Kumarbi.

In other instances, the common features are not due to cultural influences, but to the shared experiences and memories of mankind throughout the world. A typical example is the wiping out of the human race by a great flood, which is found in the mythologies of many peoples, from India to the native Americans, as well as in the Old Testament. However, the most basic single common feature of creation myths, both in Greece and throughout the world is the anxious attempt of man to explain how creation and the gods who rule it came about.

THE THEOGONY

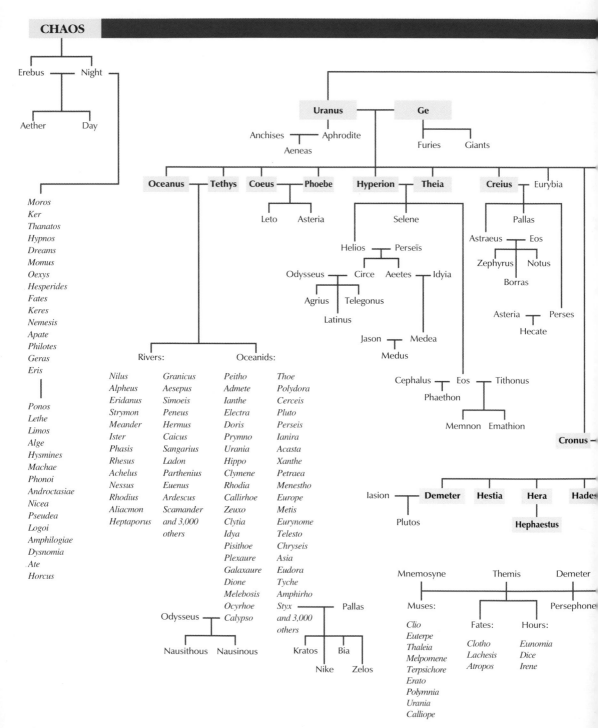

CHAOS

Erebus — Night

Aether   Day

Moros
Ker
Thanatos
Hypnos
Dreams
Momus
Oexys
Hesperides
Fates
Keres
Nemesis
Apate
Philotes
Geras
Eris

Ponos
Lethe
Limos
Alge
Hysmines
Machae
Phonoi
Androctasiae
Nicea
Pseudea
Logoi
Amphilogiae
Dysnomia
Ate
Horcus

Uranus — **Ge**

Anchises — Aphrodite
Aeneas

Furies   Giants

Oceanus — **Tethys**   **Coeus** — **Phoebe**   **Hyperion** — **Theia**   **Creius** — Eurybia

Leto   Asteria   Selene   Pallas

Helios — Perseïs   Astraeus — Eos

Odysseus — Circe   Aeetes — Idyia   Zephyrus   Notus
Borras

Agrius   Telegonus
Latinus

Asteria — Perses
Hecate

Jason — Medea
Medus

Cephalus — Eos — Tithonus
Phaethon

Memnon   Emathion

Cronus —

Rivers:

Nilus   Granicus
Alpheus   Aesepus
Eridanus   Simoeis
Strymon   Peneus
Meander   Hermus
Ister   Caicus
Phasis   Sangarius
Rhesus   Ladon
Achelus   Parthenius
Nessus   Euenus
Rhodius   Ardescus
Aliacmon   Scamander
Heptaporus   and 3,000
others

Oceanids:

Peitho   Thoe
Admete   Polydora
Ianthe   Cerceis
Electra   Pluto
Doris   Perseis
Prymno   Ianira
Urania   Acasta
Hippo   Xanthe
Clymene   Petraea
Rhodia   Menestho
Callirhoe   Europe
Zeuxo   Metis
Clytia   Eurynome
Idya   Telesto
Pisithoe   Chryseis
Plexaure   Asia
Galaxaure   Eudora
Dione   Tyche
Melebosis   Amphirho
Ocyrhoe   Styx — Pallas
    and 3,000
    others

Odysseus — Calypso

Nausithous   Nausinous

Kratos — Bia
Nike   Zelos

Iasion — **Demeter**   **Hestia**   **Hera**   **Hades**
Plutos   **Hephaestus**

Mnemosyne   Themis   Demeter

Muses: Persephone

Clio   Fates: Hours:
Euterpe
Thaleia   Clotho   Eunomia
Melpomene   Lachesis   Dice
Terpsichore   Atropos   Irene
Erato
Polymnia
Urania
Calliope

OF HESIOD

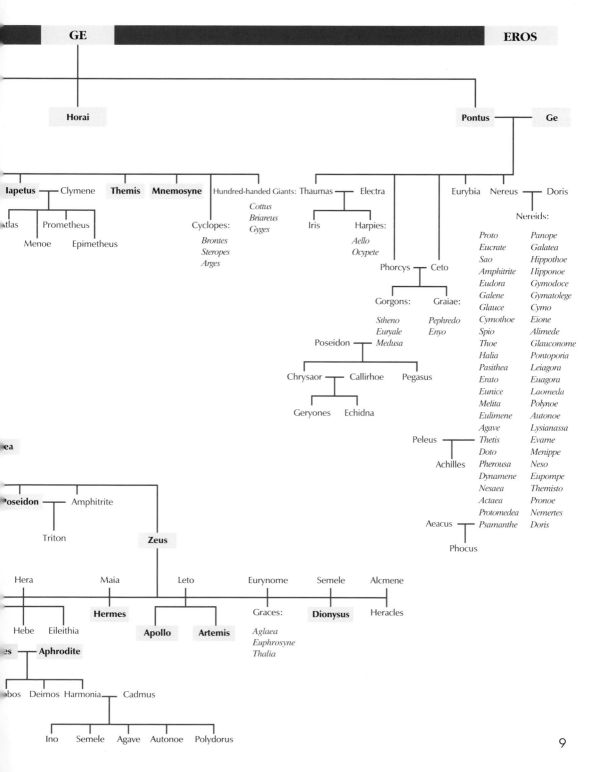

Theogony

Ge (the Earth) emerges from a chasm to rescue her son, and the son of Uranus, Polybotes, from the wrath of Poseidon, son of Rhea and Cronus. (Interior of a red-figure kylix, 420 - 400 BC).

Around 700 BC, somewhere on the slopes of Mt Helicon, the poet Hesiod gave shape to the oldest interpretation of the creation of the world and the genesis of the gods known to us: first there was Chaos, and a little afterwards the broad Earth and beautiful Eros. From Chaos were born the black Night and Erebus, who in their turn brought into the world Aether, the light of heaven, and Day.

The Earth then produced the starry Heaven to embrace it and to provide a home for the blessed gods. Also born at that time were the Mountains, on which the Nymphs disported themselves, and Pontus, the deep sea. The fruit of the union of Earth (Ge) and Heaven (Uranus) were the male and female Titans: Oceanus, Iapetus, Coeus, Creius, Hyperion, Cronus, Theia, Rhea, Mnemosyne, Themis, Phoebe, and Tethys; they were the Cyclopes Steropes, Brontes, and Arges, gigantic beings with a single round eye in the foreheads and names denoting lightning, thunder, and brightness; they were also the Hundred-handed Giants: Cottus, Gyges, and Briareos, from whose trunks sprouted a hundred hands and fifty heads.

Detail from the battle of the gods against the Giants. On the left, Nereus and Doris, and on the right, Oceanus and Tethys - the depictions are fragmentary - are defeating their demonic adversaries. (Altar of Zeus from Pergamon, northern frieze, c. 180 BC).

Other children of Night

Apart from Aether and Day, Night gave birth to numerous other children, among them Hypnos (Sleep) and Thanatos (Death), the Fates, and Nemesis, who administers justice and imposes penalties on men in accordance with their worth and their acts, Apate (Deceit), and Eris, a goddess who sows discord. The offspring of Eris were Ponos (Pain), Lethe (Oblivion), Limos (Famine), the Machae (Battles), the Phonoi (Murders), Dysnomia (Lawlessness), and Orkos (Oath) - all personifications of the relevant abstract concepts.

Ge also lay with Pontus, and gave birth to Thaumas, Eurybia, Phorcys, Ceto, and the Old Man of the Sea, Nereus. From the union of Thaumas with Electra, one of the daughters of the Titan Oceanus, the winged Iris, who, as swift as the wind, carried the messages of the gods, was born. Among the children of this couple were also the Harpies, Aello, Thyella, and Ocypete, predatory demons who stand for the destructive force of the wind and the storm. Phorcys and Ceto, who personify the monstrous forces of the deep, had as their children the two Graeae, who were born old women, and the three Gorgons Stheno, Euryale, and Medusa, demonic beings with snakes instead of hair. From the union of Nereus with Doris, another daughter of Oceanus, fifty daughters were born - the Nereids, sea deities famed for their beauty. Of the primordial trinity of the theogony of Hesiod - Chaos, the Earth, and Eros - only the latter had no descendants, but acted as an impulse which united the other forces and prompted them to creation.

Hypnos (Sleep) and Thanatos (Death), sons of Night, remove the body of a dead youth from the field of battle. (White lekythos, 440 - 435 BC).

Rhea presents Cronus with a swaddled stone instead of their child Zeus. (Red-figure pelike, c. 460 BC).

Cronus
rules the world

The Curetes seek with the clashing of their shields to disguise the crying of the new-born Zeus, whom the nymph Amalthea holds in her arms. (Architectural relief, period of Augustus).

*T*hough they were of his own blood, Uranus abhorred the Titans, and for that reason kept them imprisoned in the depths of the earth. Earth, however, who had started to fret under this weight in her bowels, resolved to take revenge on him. In this she sought the help of the Titans themselves, but only one of them, Cronus, the youngest, had the courage to carry out his mother's plans. Armed with a sharp sickle, he hid himself in the place where Uranus copulated with Ge. In the evening, when the unsuspecting Uranus held his wife in his embrace, Cronus suddenly leapt out and swiftly cut off the genitals of his father and threw them away. Thus the world's first couple were parted for ever.

From the drops of the blood of the mutilated Uranus which fell on the earth, the Giants, the Melian Nymphs, and the terrible Erinyes or Furies, who pursue those who have committed grave crimes, especially patricide and matricide, were born. From the god's genitals, which fell into the sea, Aphrodite, honoured by men, sprang up.

As soon as Cronus had come to power, he imprisoned the Cyclopes and the hundred-handed Giants and set free his brothers the Titans. Of these, the first-born, Oceanus, mated with Tethys and had three thousand sons - the rivers - and as many daughters - nymphs of springs and lakes, the Oceanids. Hyperion united himself with Theia, who

The Titan Rhea, in her efforts to preserve Zeus, the last of her children, from her husband, Cronus, who used to swallow his children so that they would not rob him of his power, gives her husband a stone wrapped in swaddling clothes. (Base, c. 160 AD).

gave birth to Helios (the Sun), Selene (the Moon), and Eos (the Dawn). Creius made Eurybia, daughter of Pontus, his wife, while Coeus married Phoebe, and Iapetus the Oceanid Clymene. Cronus himself married Rhea, but since his parents, Uranus and Ge, had told him that he would lose his power to one of his children, he took measures to prevent this: as soon as a child was born, he swallowed it at once, so that it could do him no harm.

Rhea, inconsolable because of the cruelty of her husband, sought the advice of Uranus and Ge. They took pity on her, and so, when her latest child, Zeus, was born, Ge took him and hid him in Crete, on Mt Ida. Rhea, instead of the new-born child, gave Cronus a stone wrapped in swaddling clothes, which he unsuspectingly swallowed. In the meantime, in Crete, Zeus was growing day by day, nourished by the milk of a she-goat called Amalthea. As soon as the young god felt strong enough, he went to seek out his father, wrestled with him, defeated him, and compelled him to release his brothers and sisters. From the stomach of Cronus, Demeter, Hestia, Hera, Pluto, and Poseidon emerged. The latter two, together with their brother Zeus, were to share the rule of the world.

The Nymph Amalthea

Some said that Amalthea was a nymph and that she, together with Ida, Adrastea or other nymphs brought up Zeus. The horn with which Amalthea gave milk to the young god is a symbol of plenty, of good things, of wealth - the 'cornucopia'.

The Curetes

The Curetes, warriors, but also nature demons, undertook to guard the infant Zeus. Every time that he cried, they made a loud noise by beating their swords on their shields, so that Cronus would not hear. According to one view, the Curetes are to be identified with the Corybantes, who were children of Apollo.

The battle of the Titans

The Titan Themis, daughter of Uranus and Ge. (Statue of Themis from Rhamnous, Attica, late 4th or early 3rd century BC).

*T*he children of Cronus, as soon as they emerged into the light, were filled with admiration for their noble brother Zeus and immediately sided with him against their unjust father. In the war which followed, all the deities, old and new, took part. The Titans joined the side of Cronus - though not all of them, because the terrible Oceanid Styx, together with her children Kratos (Strength), Bia (Violence), Zelos (Envy), and Nike (Victory), fought on the side of Zeus. Some say that Oceanus himself, the first-born of the Titans, and Prometheus, the son of Iapetus, supported Zeus. The headquarters of the Titans was Mt Othrys, while that of the new gods was Mt Olympus. The war lasted for twelve whole years without victory appearing to go to either side. Then it was that Ge gave an oracle to Zeus to the effect that he would be victorious only if he released the Cyclopes and the Hundred-handed Giants, whom Cronus had bound with chains in Tartara, in the depths of the earth. Zeus naturally followed her advice. The Cyclopes, now released, made a gift to Zeus of the thunder, lightning, and the thunderbolt, to Poseidon of his famous trident, and to Hades of the 'hat

An engagement in the momentous war between the Olympian gods and the Titans: Zeus brandishes his thunderbolt at a Titan, perhaps Iapetus. (Pediment of the Temple of Artemis, Corfu, c. 590 BC).

of darkness', a cap made out of the skin of a dog which made its wearer invisible. Soon the old and new allies joined battle together with renewed vigour.

A great disaster followed. Zeus thundered and lightened, the earth burned and the waters of the ocean boiled. In the end, it was the Hundred-handed Giants who decided the outcome of the war. They siezed three hundred huge rocks in their three hundred hands and threw them at the Titans, crushing them beneath them. The Titans now surrendered and were hurled into Tartara. It was said to take nine days and nine nights for a bronze anvil to reach Tartara from the surface of the earth, and it took that long for the Titans to reach their place of imprisonment. There the Hundred-handed Giants, sent by Zeus, faithful and eternal sentinels, awaited them, to ensure that they would never again see the light of the sun.

The Titan Atlas supports on his shoulders the sphere of the earth. (The 'Farnese Atlas', 2nd century BC).

Atlas

Atlas, the son of the Titan Iapetus and the Oceanid Clymene, angered Zeus either because during the Battle of the Titans he had supported the Titans, or because he and his brothers Menoetius, Prometheus, and Epimetheus had scorned the new leader of the gods. Thus he was condemned to support the heavens or the heavens and the earth on his shoulders for all eternity. Of his children, the Pleiades, seven girls of great beauty, were changed into stars, the constellation of Poulia or the Pleiades, because they could not bear to see their father punished in this way. Another myth relates that Atlas was the first-born son of Poseidon. His father made him king of a mythical island, beyond the Ocean, which took his name: Atlantis.

15

Fate, the constant supporter of Zeus in the Battle of the Giants, fights against a monstrous Giant. (Altar of Zeus from Pergamon, northern frieze, c. 180 BC).

The battle of the Giants

*T*he Giants were born from the blood of the mutilated Uranus, or, according to another version, they were brought into the world by Ge, either because she was angry about the harsh punishment of the Titans, or because the gods did not honour her as they should. These enormous beings had human form, but with a trunk which ended in a dragon's tail, and with snakes for the hair and beard. Their strength was unimaginable, even though they did not belong to the world of the immortals.

The attack of the Giants on the gods of Olympus, which began on the instigation of their mother or on their own initiative, was a sudden one. A rain of rocks and burning trees suddenly struck Olympus. Earth and heaven were confused together, islands sank, rivers changed their course, the whole world was transformed into a hell.

Then the gods entered the battle, led by Zeus. Fighting alongside him in the front line were his brothers and his children - Apollo, Hephaestus, Athena. Although the gods of Olympus fought hard, the Giants showed no sign of yielding and the battle did not look as though it would be easily won.

At this critical moment, it became known that the gods would win only if they recruited some mortal to their ranks. Zeus immediately sent Athena to bring to Olympus his beloved son Heracles. Ge - the Earth - for her part set about looking for some herb which would save the Giants. Zeus, how-

Zeus, in the centre, Athena, on the right, and Artemis, on the left, fight the enemies of Zeus, the Giants. (Red-figure kylix, 420 - 400 BC).

Scene from a large composition depicting the Battle of the Giants. On the left, Athena has seized the Giant Alcyoneus by the hair. On the right, his mother, Ge, emerges from a chasm, begging for the life of her son. Nike (Victory) flies towards Athena to crown her. (Altar of Zeus from Pergamon, eastern frieze, c. 180 BC).

In this composition, the Battle of the Giants is shown as a conflict of cosmic forces. Two Giants are holding enormous rocks, the mountains of Pelion and Ossa (?). Ge (the Earth) rises from a chasm and watches her children with concern. Above, Helios (the Sun), in his chariot, rises in the firmament. (Red-figure krater, 400 - 390 BC).

A battle of the gods against the Giants. Zeus raises his thunderbolt, while Hera attacks her enemies with her spear. Athena and Nike (Victory) support Zeus. (Detail from a red-figure krater, c. 440 BC).

ever, forbade the Sun, the Moon, and the Dawn to make their appearance before he, under cover of darkness, had himself found the herb and removed it. As soon as Zeus had achieved his purpose, the gods began to drive back the Giants.

First of all, Heracles killed Alcyoneus, the leader of the Giants. Enceladus was pursued by Athena all over the Mediterranean; in the end, she beat him down and hurled the whole of Sicily on top of him. Poseidon cut off a piece of Cos with his trident and with it crushed Polybotes. Thus the island of Nisyros was formed, with the Giant buried beneath it. The terrible Ephialtes was shot with the arrows of Apollo and Heracles. But most of the Giants were wiped out by Zeus with his thunderbolts and by Heracles with his deadly bow. Soon, of the hundred or so Giants, not a single one was left.

The Battle of the Giants and natural phenomena

The myth of the Battle of the Giants echoes memories of violent natural phenomena such as storms and whirlwinds, droughts and fires, earthquakes and floods. The volcanic activity of Vesuvius, Etna, and Nisyros was attributed to the wrath of the Giants, who lay buried in the bowels of the earth. Even the fossils of prehistoric beasts discovered by the ancients were believed to be the bones of the Giants.

Typhon

Zeus hurls his thunderbolt against the powerful monster Typhon, the terrible demon born by Ge (the Earth) to avenge the death of her children the Giants. (Chalcis hydria, 540 - 530 BC).

The monster Typhon. (Interior of a Laconian black-figure kylix, attributed to the Typhon Painter, 560 - 555 BC).

*T*he slaughter of the Giants angered Ge. In order to take her revenge on the gods, she lay with Tartarus and gave birth, in Cilicia, to Typhon. This fearful monster was stronger than all Earth's children. From the waist up he had the form of a man, and from the waist down, that of a dragon. A hundred dragon heads sprouted from his shoulders and vipers from his legs, while his whole body was covered with feathers. His head touched the stars, and when he stretched out his arms, one reached to the extremity of the West and the other to the extremity of the East. His voice resembled the lowing of a bull, the roaring of a lion, or the barking of a dog; sometimes it took the form of hammer-beats which made the mountains reverberate.

As soon as the gods became aware of the arrival of Typhon, they changed themselves into various animals and hastened to hide in Egypt. Of all the immortals, only Zeus and his intrepid daughter Athena remained at their stations, determined to deal with this new threat. Zeus began to strike at Typhon from a distance with his thunderbolts and at close hand with the sickle with which Ge had armed the hand of Cronus against his father, Uranus. When the monster began to retreat, Zeus took courage and rushed upon him. Typhon, however, wrapped

his snake tails round the body of Zeus, and, having succeeded in taking the sickle from him, used it to cut the tendons from his arms and legs. He then took the god, unconscious, to Cilicia, where he threw him into a cave, the Corycian Cave. He wrapped the tendons of Zeus in a bear's skin, hid them in the cave, and set a she-dragon, Delphyne, to guard them.

In the end, the situation was saved by Zeus's cunning son Hermes, and Aegipan, that is, the god Pan transformed into a goat. After immense difficulties, they succeeded in stealing the tendons of the father of the gods and restoring them to his body. As soon as Zeus recovered, he launched a sudden attack on Typhon from the sky, riding in a chariot drawn by winged horses. After a long pursuit, the monster reached a mountain range in Thrace. A hard battle followed, and the whole mountain range took the name of Haimos from the blood (*haima*) of the wounded Typhon, which flowed like a river. Finally, as Typhon rushed towards Sicily to escape, Zeus hurled Etna on top of him and crushed him. It was said that the flames of the volcano are due to the innumerable thunderbolts which Zeus launched in this battle.

The children of Typhon

From the union of Typhon with Echidna, who was half woman and half snake, many monsters were born: the dog Orthus, Cerberus, the guard-dog of Hades, the Lernaean Hydra, the Chimaera, Scylla, the dragon which guarded the Apples of the Hesperides, the dragon which guarded the Golden Fleece of Cholcis, the Sphinx, and the eagle which ate the liver of Prometheus. The furious winds were also the children of Typhon.

Myth and historical events

Perhaps in the flight of the gods to Egypt we find imprinted on the myth of Typhon memories of hasty movements of Helladic populations to Africa, probably made during the course of some unusual volcanic activity, such as the tremendous eruption of the volcano of Thera, around 1450 BC.

The races of man

Epimetheus liberating with his hammer Pandora, the first woman in the world, the mother of Deucalion and Pyrrha. Pandora is approached by Hermes, on the orders of Zeus, who stands on the left, in order to give her a flower. (Red-figure krater, c. 450 BC).

A ccording to Hesiod, there were five human races, and these were created by the gods, each after the disappearance of the preceding one. The first human race created by the immortals was the golden one, which lived in the reign of Cronus. At that time, human beings led a happy life, without pain or sorrow, enjoying the good things which the earth abundantly provided of its own accord; and when all this generation was covered by the earth, they were transformed into good spirits, guardians and saviours of mankind. The next race, the silver one, was not perfect, as the first had been. These men were foolish and did not honour the gods as they should. For this reason, Zeus, who by now ruled the world, wiped them out and created a third generation, the race of bronze. It was with these men that wars and violence made their appearance. In this generation,

the weapons and the houses were made of bronze. The fourth race to live on earth was the heroic one. It was made up of the demi-gods who fought below the walls of Thebes, and of those who travelled to distant Troy to bring back the fair Helen. These heroes live eternally on the Islands of the Blest, a happy place where the sun shines day and night and the earth gives its fruit three times a year. The fifth and

Near the metalworking Cyclopes we see Deucalion and Pyrrha, the authors of the new human race, after the flood sent by Zeus to wipe out the bronze generation of men for their lawlessness. (Sarcophagus, c. 270 AD).

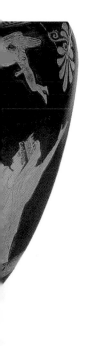

last race of man is the iron one, a generation tormented by cares and woes. It is this which the poet wishes he had never known, but that he had died before it or been born after it.

Another myth tells us that at one time men became so evil that Zeus resolved to bring about a terrible flood to wipe them out. However, Prometheus warned his son Deucalion, who constructed an ark in which he, his wife, Pyrrha, the daughter of Epimetheus and Pandora, escaped. As soon as the rain stopped and the waters subsided, the couple made a sacrifice to Zeus to thank him for their survival. The god was now satisfied and told Deucalion and Pyrrha to ask whatever favour they wished, and they sought the favour of human beings. Zeus instructed them to begin to walk, with their faces covered, throwing stones behind them. Where the stones thrown by Deucalion fell, the earth produced men. Where those of Pyrrha fell, it produced women. Thus a whole new people was created.

Deucalion and Pyrrha had their own children, from whom many local eponymous heroes were descended. Of their first-born, Hellen, the ancestor of the Hellenes, it is said that he was really the son of Zeus and not of Deucalion.

The 'double' race

According to a myth recorded by Plato, the first race of mankind consisted of three sexes: one male, one female, and a third which was was both male and female. Those of all three sexes had a round body and double the number of members - that is, two faces, four legs, four hands. These first human beings, however, became so arrogant that Zeus decided to divide each of them into two pieces, to reduce their strength. From that point on, human beings, since they feel themselves to be only a half person, seek by making love to unite themselves with their other half.

Prometheus, the benefactor of mankind

Part of a composition showing the creation of the human race. Athena breathes life into newly-formed man, who is held by Prometheus, who has fashioned him. On the pedestal, man stands in a state of dejection. (Sarcophagus, c. 270 AD).

*T*he races of mortals, one myth tells us, were made by the gods in the earth, from earth and fire. A little before they brought them to the light, they called upon Prometheus and Epimetheus, the sons of the Titan Iapetus, and told them to adorn them and distribute gifts among them. Epimetheus, however, wanted to make the distribution himself and his brother agreed to this. So Epimetheus began with the animals. To some he gave strength, to others swiftness. To some he gave great size, while the small ones he provided with an underground home or the ability to fly. And, in order to make sure that none of them should become extinct, he clothed them with thick coats and gave them the appropriate equipment. But since Epimetheus was not particularly wise, he forgot to leave any gift for the race of man. While he was wondering what to do, Prometheus arrived to inspect the distribution. And so he found all the animals equipped and adorned, and man naked and unprotected. Prometheus thought about the problem and decided on a course of action. He stole fire from the gods, with all the skills related to it, so that with this provision man could survive. It was

Two of the Titans, Atlas in the West and Prometheus in the East, were punished by Zeus for their hostility towards him. Atlas, on the left, is bowed under the weight of the heavens, which he has been sentenced to hold up on his shoulders, while, on the right, Prometheus is tormented by the wounds inflicted by the eagle. (Laconian kylix, c. 550 BC).

Prometheus was honoured by torch races in Attica. In this depiction, Satyrs hold torches as they dance, astounded by the gift of Prometheus, who stands by holding the stick from which the fire hidden within it emerges. (Red-figure krater, 420 - 410 BC).

Prometheus stands before the enthroned Hera, who welcomes him to Olympus. Their names are given. (Interior of a red-figure kylix, 480 - 470 BC).

said, moreover, that it was Prometheus who taught man all the arts and sciences. Other accounts say that it was Prometheus himself who made mankind, alone, or with the help of Athena.

According to yet another myth, when the gods and men met to decide upon the rights of each, Prometheus deceived Zeus. He slaughtered an ox and cut the skin in two. In one of the pieces he wrapped up all the lean meat and in the other the fat and the bones and put the two before the god for him to choose between them. Zeus chose the half with the bones in it, and then Prometheus gave the other to mankind. Thus it became established practice for men to burn the fat and bones of sacrifices as an offering to the gods and to eat the meat themselves.

Prometheus paid dearly for his goodness towards mankind and his lack of respect for Zeus. He was condemned to be tied to a stake on the summit of the Caucasus. Every day an eagle descended upon him and ate his liver, which was then renewed, so that the next day the eagle could come and eat it again. Thirty years later, Heracles came to the spot, and with the permission of Zeus released Prometheus from his torment.

Pandora

When Zeus discovered that Prometheus had stolen fire, he was extremely angry. In order to punish mankind, he told Hephaestus to make a woman out of earth and water. To this woman each of the gods gave a gift - some beauty, some skill, and so on - and for this reason the woman was called Pandora ('All Gifts'). Hermes, however, on the orders of Zeus, put wickedness into the soul of Pandora and took her to Epimetheus, supposedly as a gift from the gods. One day, Pandora, out of curiosity, opened a storage jar which the gods had entrusted to her, whereupon all the ills and disasters which torment mankind leapt out. Last, at the bottom of the jar, only Elpis - Hope - remained.

THE GODS

ZEUS, father of gods
and men

*G*iven that the ancient Greeks tended to personify every natural phenomenon and every abstract concept, Greek mythology is particularly rich in gods and demons. Above all other deities the people honoured the Twelve Gods of Olympus, who were worshipped collectively, over and above the worship offered to each one individually.

The list of the Twelve Gods varies from place to place. Its most familiar form includes: **Zeus, Hera, Athena, Poseidon, Demeter, Apollo, Artemis, Hermes, Ares, Aphrodite, Hephaestus, Hestia**. In some areas, the place of Hestia, the highly respectable goddess who protected the home and the family, is taken by Dionysus.

HERA, first lady of
Olympus

In the share-out of the cosmos which took place by lot among the three sons of Cronus, Zeus was recognised as lord of the heavens, Poseidon as lord of the waters, and Pluto as ruler of the Underworld.

The dwelling-place of the Twelve Gods was cloudless Olympus, bathed in eternal light. It was there that they had their palaces, it was there that they passed their time dancing, eating ambrosia and drinking nectar.

APHRODITE, goddess of
beauty and of love

Of great personal beauty, the immortals lived 'in the image and likeness' of mortals. They had love affairs, they were jealous, they fell out, they took offence, they burst into laughter on the slightest provocation. Unlike men, however, they were free not only of death but of any material or moral constraint. They enjoyed life and committed crimes without the fear that one day they would have to pay for them. The only form of commit-

ARTEMIS, goddess of
hunting

HERMES, messenger of
the gods

POSEIDON, ruler of the seas

APOLLO, god of light

ment which they recognised was an oath on the waters of the Styx, the sacred river of the Underworld. The water for this was brought to Olympus in a silver cup by the swift-footed Iris. If the god who swore by this violated his oath, he was bereft of breath for a whole year and was unable to touch either nectar or ambrosia. He then remained segregated from the other gods for nine years, and only in the tenth was he accepted again in the palaces of Olympus.

In spite of the carefree character of the gods, they were profoundly respected by mortals and were felt to be close to human beings at every turn in their lives. Their justice was also trusted. In very serious cases, such as differences between immortal beings or very grave crimes, only the Twelve Gods could give judgment.

The major gods of Olympus were flanked by a whole army of lesser divinities - gods of the earth, the sea, the heavens, or of the Underworld, who also received their share of honours and intervened in the life of men - for good or ill.

DEMETER, protector of agriculture

HEPHAESTUS, god of metalworking

HESTIA, protector of family life

ARES, god of war

ATHENA, goddess of wisdom

Zeus,
father of gods and men

Zeus, lord of the heavens, flourishes his thunderbolt, ready to hurl it from the heights of Olympus to earth.
(Bronze statuette of 'Keraunios' Zeus from Dodona, 470 - 460 BC).

*F*irst among the gods was the imposing, the magnificent Zeus. From his palace on Olympus he ruled the world and imposed his will on gods and mortals. A god of the heavens par excellence, as is shown by many of the epithets applied to him, Zeus was responsible for all changes in the weather. It was he who sent to the earth rain, hail, snow, thunderbolts, and lightning, which were sometimes good omens and sometimes bad. His symbols were the thunderbolt and the eagle, a bird unique in the heights it attains in the sky and, which when it wishes to snatch up a victim, swoops to the earth like lightning.

Zeus was invoked by men on many occasions. As Zeus Herkeios (*herkos* = fence) he protected the house and its courtyard. The head of the family offered sacrifice on its altar, which was located in the courtyard. Strangers, the poor and refugees were also under the protection of Zeus, a fact reflected in his titles of Zeus Xenios, Ikesios, Phyxios. Also held in admiration was the justice of Zeus. It was to this that the gods had recourse when there was some dispute between them, and men called upon him to take care of their rights. Zeus, by his unerring judg-

Zeus, the lord of Olympus, sits with his wife, Hera, on his throne, holding the symbols of his power and might: the sceptre, the eagle, and the thunderbolt. Iris, the winged messenger of the gods, stands before the divine couple with a wine-pourer and a bowl for libations. (Red-figure amphora, c. 500 BC).

Bronze statuette of 'Keraunios' Zeus with his thunderbolt in one hand and lightning in the other. (Bronze statuette of 'Keraunios' Zeus from Dodona, 530 - 520 BC).

The origins of Zeus

Zeus seems to have been an extremely ancient god of the heavens, the worship of whom was introduced by the Hellenes when they arrived in the Balkan peninsula around 2000 BC. The name is derived from the root 'div', meaning 'heaven', 'sky', and is encountered among other Indo-European peoples, such as the Indians and the Latins. This means that he had been worshipped at least since the third millennium BC, when these peoples were still united and spoke the same language. It is significant that the Greek 'Zeus pater' corresponds to the 'Diespiter' (Jupiter) of the Romans and the 'Dyaous Piter' of the ancient Indians.

ment, settled all these differences without causing displeasure to either side.

The family life of Zeus seems to have been troubled. Some relate that his first wife was Chthonie, whom he named Ge, and that it was for her sake that he made the world. Again, it is said that he united himself with one of the daughters of Oceanus, Metis, who had in her mind all the wisdom of the gods and of men. When Zeus heard that Metis would give birth to a daugher, and then to a son, who would rob him of his power, he swallowed her. Metis, however, was already pregnant with Athena, who, nine months later, sprang fully-armed from the head of her father. Another tradition maintains that his first wife was the Oceanid Dione, who bore him a daughter - Aphrodite. However, his sister Hera was regarded as the lawful and permanent wife of Zeus. Their children were Ares, Hephaestus, Hebe, goddess of sweet youth, and Eileithyia, who protected women in childbirth. The life of this divine couple resembled the life of a mortal patriarchal family. There was no shortage of quarrels and fits of anger, but in spite of this, Zeus and Hera shared the same bed each night as a loving couple.

On this coin from Dodona in Epirus, Zeus is shown with his first wife, Dione. (Two-drachma coin of the Commune of the Epirots, 230 - 220 BC).

27

The love life of Zeus

*T*he love affairs of Zeus were truly innumerable. The father of gods and men loved many goddesses, who presented him with fine children such as Artemis and Apollo (by Leto) and Hermes (by Maia). With Mnemosyne, the daughter of Uranus and Ge, Zeus slept for nine successive nights. When the time came for Mnemosyne to give birth, she produced the nine Muses, the patrons of letters and the arts. At festivals on Olympus, the Muses would accompany the cithara of Apollo with their divine song, under the proud gaze of their father. The dance was led by the three Graces, Euphrosyne, Thalia, and Aegle, who were also daughters of Zeus, and of the Oceanid Eurynome. The role of cupbearer was played by the young Ganymede, a prince of Troy with whom Zeus had fallen in love and taken to Olympus.

The three Fates were the result of Zeus' liaison with the Titan Themis, goddess of justice. Their names were Clotho, who wove the thread of the life of each human being, Lachesis, who determined what fate would fall to his lot, and Atropos, who cut the thread of life. Their sisters were the three Hours, Eunomia, Dike, and Eirene, kindly divinities who opened and closed the gates of the heavens. Since it was they who made time roll on, they also brought to man the fruits of his labours.

But the mortals who were the object of the desire of the king of gods were also without

Zeus attempts to make advances to a young woman, perhaps the nymph Aegina, while she runs away in fear to escape his clutches. (Red-figure hydria, c. 490 BC).

Here the god attempts to embrace his beloved Ganymede, son of King Tros, who resists in alarm. (Interior of a red-figure kylix, c. 460 BC).

number. Among them were Alcmene, who gave him a son - Heracles - Danae, mother of Perseus, and Aegina, mother of Aeacus. This intense erotic activity on the part of Zeus had a rational explanation. The nobles of the Archaic era claimed to be descended from Zeus, so they took care to have at the beginning of their family tree some mortal girl of noble birth whose beauty had prompted the god to want to make her his own. This was the real reason why Zeus was reported to have so many mortal mistresses. In order to win the girls whom he desired, Zeus employed a variety of devices. In the case of Europa, the ravishing daughter of Agenor, King of Phoenicia, he changed himself into a bull and made his appearance in the meadow where the girl was playing with her friends. As soon as she saw him, she was struck by his beauty and began to stroke him; she then climbed on his back, whereupon the bull galloped off across the sea and took her to Crete, where he made love to her. Europa was to bear Zeus three sons - Minos, Sarpedon, and Rhadamanthus - and to give her name to an entire continent.

29

Hera fights against the Giants, together with the other gods. Here she charges with her spear against a Giant. (Red-figure kylix, 420 - 400 BC).

Hera, first lady of Olympus

Hera was one of the most respected of the goddesses of Greece. The radiantly beautiful first lady of Olympus is shown here with sumptuous garments, a royal diadem, and a sceptre. (Interior of a kylix with a white background, 470 - 460 BC).

At the side of Zeus was Hera, one of the most respected divinities of ancient Greece. The Queen of Olympus was the protectress of marriage and of women, whether unmarried, married, or widows. Tradition says that the divine couple had premarital relations. Zeus, who had long been attempting to 'get her on her own', had his opportunity when he saw her climbing a mountain all alone. He brought about a sudden downpour, changed himself into a cuckoo, and sat shivering on her knee. Hera took pity on the bird and covered it with the edge of her dress. At once the god resumed his real form in order to make love to her. To begin with, Hera resisted, because she was afraid that her mother, Rhea, would be angry, but she yielded when Zeus promised her that he would make her his lawful wife. From that point the cuckoo became a cult symbol of the goddess.

Hera, provocatively beautiful, presents herself before Zeus, who summons her to him. (Wall-painting from the 'House of the Tragic Poet' at Pompeii, c. 75 AD).

Hera protected those who honoured her, but was harsh and vengeful towards those who did not reckon with her power or wronged the weak and the defenceless. She was particularly relentless in pursuing the mistresses and bastards of her husband. When Leto was pregnant with Apollo and Artemis, she would not allow her to give birth. She changed the nymph Callisto, in Arcadia, into a bear and let her be killed by Artemis, or by her own son, Arcadas. In the case of Heracles, she made him pay for the whole of his life for the love of his father, Zeus, for him.

At one point, Hera, tired of her husband's infidelities, made up her mind to leave him. She took refuge in Euboea and refused to return, in spite of the pleadings of Zeus. However, Cithaeron, a wise king, advised him to take a wooden statue, dress it as a bride, and put about the story that he was getting married. As soon as she heard this, Hera hastened back, rushed up to the carriage and tore the veil of the 'bride'. When she realised that she had been tricked, she enjoyed a good laugh, and was reconciled with the king of the gods.

Io

One of the girl-friends of Zeus, Io, daughter of Inachus, was changed by Hera into a heifer and was tied to an olive tree in the grove of Mycenae. The monster Argos, whose body was covered with eyes, was set to watch her. When Hermes, sent by Zeus, succeeded in releasing her, Hera sent a gadfly, which began to bite Io, driving her, maddened, from place to place. She crossed the Ionian Sea, which took its name from her, and after many wanderings arrived in Egypt. There she recovered her human form and was able to give birth to her son Epaphus, the future King of Egypt.

31

Athena,
goddess of wisdom

Bronze statue of Athena, probably the work of Euphranor, c. 350 BC.

Athena, the goddess renowned for her valour and intelligence, was born from the head of her father, Zeus. Her mother was Metis, goddess of prudence, whom Zeus swallowed when he was told by Uranus and Ge that she would give birth first to a daughter and then a son who would take the throne from him. When the time came for Athena to see the light of day, Zeus told Prometheus - or Hephaestus - to split his head open with an axe. Then, before the astonished eyes of all the gods, she leapt out, uttering a savage battle cry and with all her weapons in her hands, the wise daughter of Zeus.

In the Attica region the story was told that once Poseidon had a quarrel with Athena as to who should take under his or her protection the beautiful city of Athens, which at that time was known as Cecropia, after a very ancient indigenous King, Cecrops. The two deities agreed that whichever of them gave it the best gift would win the city. Poseidon struck the ground with his trident, creating a rift from which water gushed. Athena, in her turn, kicked the earth and the first olive tree in the world sprang up. The other gods, as judges of the contest, awarded the victory to Athena, who gave her name to the city. Athena, though a war goddess, knew how to combine courage with cunning. Unlike her bloodthirsty brother Ares, she always helped those whom she favoured to achieve their purposes without needless bloodshed. The epithets applied to her demonstrate the role which she played in the life of man. As Athena Promachos she gave her assistance in battle and supported him in difficult situations. Many heroes, such as Perseus, Heracles, Jason, and, above, all her favourite Odysseus, were delivered from dangers of every kind thanks to her advice. She also concerned herself with the safety of young warri-

The birth of Athena.
(Black-figure amphora of the
E Group, c. 550 BC).

Figurine of Athena,
height approx. 17 cm.
The goddess is seated
on a throne, with a
'polos' head-dress
and the aegis and
gorgoneion on her
breast.
(Figurine of Athena of
the Archaic period).

ors and of their generation, and for that reason she was called 'Soteira' (Saviour).

Athena also made her presence felt in the life of mortals in peacetime. As the daughter of Metis, she was a goddess of wisdom. She protected poets, orators, and philosophers. Her skill in such arts as ceramics or woodwork, which she taught to mankind, explained yet another epithet given to her: Ergane (from a root meaning 'work'). There was a particularly strong connection between Athena and weaving. She wove the very first textiles, and it was she who made the Phaeacian women unrivalled in the art of the loom. A myth in this connection tells of a young woman from Libya, Arachne, who was so skilled in the weaving of carpets that she challenged the goddess to a competition. Athena, enraged either that a mortal should dare to compare herself with her, or because the girl had depicted the love affairs of the gods in her works, changed her into a spider.

Athena was frequently referred to as Pallas, which means a young girl and is connected with the Modern Greek word *pallekari* (a gallant youth) (Ancient Greek *pallax*). The Athenians called her simply 'the Virgin' (Parthenos), and for that reason the temple built in her honour on the Acropolis took the name of the Parthenon.

Erichthonius

One day Athena went into the smithy of Hephaestus to order new weapons. As soon as he saw her, Hephaestus felt a strong desire for her, but Athena, who wished to remain a virgin, ran away. Hephaestus chased her and came close to her; although he did not manage to have his way with her, his seed fell on her leg. The goddess wiped herself with a tuft of wool and threw it to the ground. In this way the earth was fertilised and gave birth to Erichthonius (from *erion* = wool, and *chthon* = the earth), one of the early indigenous kings of Athens.

Poseidon, lord of the seas

Poseidon, ruler of the seas, is shown here brandishing his trident (which has not survived). (Bronze statue of the 'Poseidon of Artemisium', c. 460 BC).

*T*he revered brother of Zeus, Poseidon, was the deity responsible for stirring up the waters with his trident, and, again with his trident, for soothing them again, thus granting calm to those who sailed on the oceans. The ancients believed that he was also responsible for a whole series of geological phenomena, such as earthquakes, and for that reason they sought his intervention to secure the stability of the earth and the safety of buildings.

Like the rest of the Olympians, Poseidon had his palace on the summit of the sacred mountain of Olympus. His true kingdom, however, was in the depths of the sea, where there awaited him a second palace made of glittering gold. There he spent his days and nights in the company of his wife, Amphitrite, one of the fifty alluring daughters of Nereus. As god of the sea, Poseidon travelled over the waves, which joyfully parted as he passed, in a golden chariot, while dolphins sported around him.

Following the example of Zeus, Poseidon enjoyed the favours of great goddessses and beautiful mortal girls. According to one tradition, the god grew up on Rhodes, the home of the Telchines, sons of the sea and highly skilled craftsmen and inventors. The first of his loves was the sister of the Telchines, Alia, who bore him six sons and a daughter, Rhode, from whom the island took its name. Poseidon had many other children, among them great he-

The venerable Poseidon is shown here in a hieratic pose, calm and with his trident resting on the ground. (Black-figure amphora, 540 - 530 BC).

Bronze statuette of Poseidon. The trident is a modern addition (second half of the 2nd century BC).

Bronze statuette of Poseidon of the late Hellenistic period, a copy of a work by Lysippus.

roes such as Theseus, but also savage rulers or robbers, such as Procrustes and Sciro, who were active in the Attica region.

It is also said that from his union with Iphimedea, daughter of the King of Thessaly, he had twin sons, the handsome giants Otus and Ephialtes, who swore that they would make two great goddesses, Artemis and Hera, their own. In order to punish them, Artemis lured them to Naxos. There she changed herself into a deer and stood in a position between them. They took aim at her, but just as they were hurling their spears, the animal disappeared and the two brothers slew each other. With Elara, daughter of Orchomenus, Poseidon had another son of gigantic stature, Tityus, who attempted to rape Leto and was killed by Zeus or Apollo. The giant Orion was also held to be his son, by Euryale, daughter of Minos. Famed for his good looks and a fine hunter, Orion had the gift of being able to walk on the waves. After his death by a scorpion's bite, he was changed by Zeus into a constellation, with Scorpio at his feet, to remind mortals of his end.

Sea demons

A large number of sea demons also inhabited the kingdom of Poseidon. The most important among them were Proteus, Triton, and Glaucus, who were said by some to be the children of Poseidon and Amphitrite. Proteus possessed the magic power of turning himself into whatever animal he wished, or even into the elements of nature, such as wind or fire. Trition was half man and half fish and was employed in looking after the horses and chariot of his father. He had the habit of blowing on conches and thus filling the sea with harmonious sounds and of amusing himself with his swimming and with flirting with the Nereids. In the case of Glaucus, who was imagined as having seaweed and shells all over his body, seamen believed that he had the gift of prophecy.

Demeter,
patron of farming

Demeter. From the northern frieze of the Altar of Zeus from Pergamon, c. 180 BC.

*T*his very ancient goddess of fertility was the protectress of work in the fields and was worshipped chiefly by countryfolk. The Modern Greek word for cereals (*demetria-ka*) is derived from her name (*da* = 'the earth' and 'mother').

An allegorical myth makes Pluto the son of Demeter. She bore him after her union with the hero Iasion, in Crete, in a field which had been ploughed three times.

Demeter was also desired by Poseidon, but to avoid him, she took the form of a mare; but the god promptly changed himself into a stallion and mated with her. As a result, she bore the divine horse Arion, and a daughter whose name was unknown to those not initiated into the Mysteries.

Demeter's favourite daughter, however, was the fruit of her union with Zeus - Persephone. This girl was so beautiful that when Pluto - or Hades - the god of the Underworld, saw her, he resolved to abduct her. One day, when Persephone was picking flowers with her friends the Oceanids, Zeus, acting as Pluto's accomplice, asked Ge - the Earth - to help them, and she caused a delightful narcissus to spring up. The girl, unsuspecting, went to pick the wonderful flower, but at that very moment the earth opened and from its depths Pluto emerged in his chariot and carried her off in his embrace. At the time when Persephone disappeared from the face of the earth, the rocks and the mountains sent to her mother the reverberations of herlaments.

For nine days Demeter searched the whole world, out of her mind with grief and worry. In the end, the goddess Hecate, who had also heard these sounds, took her to Helios

Pluto and Persephone on a four-horse chariot which hastens towards the country of the dead. In front of them Hecate lights their path, while Hermes follows them.
(Apulian krater, 360 - 350 BC).

Triptolemus, sitting in a winged chariot, looks at Persephone, who is holding a burning torch and a wine-pourer for oblations. Behind Triptolemus, Demeter also holds a torch and ears of wheat.
(Red-figure skyphos, c. 480 BC).

- the Sun - who sees everything from heaven. He was moved with pity for her and revealed the identity of the abductor. Outraged by the behaviour of Zeus, the goddess left Olympus and began to roam hither and thirther, until she came to Eleusis. There, disguised as a mortal, she looked after the new-born son of King Celeus, Demophon. In order to reward the hospitality which she had received, Demeter wished to make Demophon immortal by holding him in the fire at nights. One night, however, Metaneira, the child's mother, happened to see her doing this and, terrified, began to scream. The goddess then revealed her true identity, and the inhabitants of Eleusis built a temple to her. Demeter shut herself indoors, mourning the loss of her beautiful daughter, and nothing grew from the earth any more.

When Zeus learnt of all this, he ordered his brother to let Persephone go. He agreed, but before she went, he gave her a pomegranate seed to eat, which meant that she was bound to return to him. Finally, both sides reached an agreement. Four months of the year Persephone spent with her husband and eight in the world above, with her mother, who was now content to let the earth bear fruit again.

The Eleusinian Mysteries

The Mysteries were rites which took place every October at Eleusis, commemorating the ascent of Persephone from the Underworld. No one knows exactly what took place in the Hall of Initiation, in the torchlight. The only thing which we know is that the initiates believed that a better life was awaiting them in the world below.

Triptolemus

Triptolemus was King of Eleusis. With the help of Demeter and Persephone, he made the first plough and learnt how to use it, how to sow seed, and how to reap and thresh. At a later stage, he began to wander the earth, teaching mankind the cultivation of cereals.

Apollo,
god of light

*L*eto, daughter of the Titans Coeus and Phoebe, at some point became pregnant by Zeus. But there was no place which would receive
her so that she could give birth, since they all feared the rage of the
jealous Hera. After wandering over almost the whole of Greece,
she came at last to the obscure and barren island of Delos.
Leto's promise that the son whom she was about to bear
would lend eternal glory to the island induced it to accept
her.

For nine days Leto was in agonising travail. Only Eileithyia, goddess of childbirth, could have helped her,
but she was sitting unconcerned on Olympus because
Hera had ringed her with golden clouds so that she
would see and hear nothing. Fortunately, the swift-
footed Iris came to her secretly and, with the inducement of a necklace woven with gold
threads, persuaded her to follow her.

As soon as Eileithyia set foot on the island, Leto brought Apollo into the world. To their
astonishment, the goddesses who stood by his mother saw him grow up in a few minutes.
And Delos, delighted to have been deemed worthy of such an honour, shone with gold.
One of the first decisions which the god took was to set up an oracle, a place where
mortals could discover from the mouths of priests the will of his father, Zeus. Thus, one
day, he left Olympus and began the search for the place where the oracle would be sit-
ed. After many adventures, he arrived at a sheer side of Mt Parnassus, where Delphi
stands today. There, next to a spring, he slew Pytho, a huge snake, which devoured any
man or beast who passed that way. For this reason the god was known as Pythian Apol-

*Detail of the statue of
Apollo which dominates
the centre of the Battle of
the Centaurs depicted on
the pediment of the Temple
of Zeus at Olympia.
(Statue of Apollo from the
western pediment of the
Temple of Zeus at
Olympia, c. 457 BC).*

Apollo is shown playing the cithara, between his mother, Leto, and his sister, Artemis. (Red-figure amphora, late 6th century BC).

Leto on Delos, sitting on a stool, with her head bowed and an expression of pain on her face, rests her hand on a palm tree, and is about to give birth. Behind her is Eileithyia, and in front of her Athena and the other goddesses lend their support. (Red-figure pyxis, c. 370 BC).

Apollo with his bow and quiver on his back and striking his lyre is travelling over the sea towards Delphi, seated on the tripod of the oracle, which is here shown winged. (Red-figure hydria, 480 - 470 BC)

lo. Here he laid the foundations of the temple of an oracle, whose fame was to reach the ends of the earth.

A little later, as he was looking out to sea from on high, Apollo spotted a ship taking Cretans to Pylos. He immediately changed himself into a dolphin, and leapt on to the deck. The ship took itself of its own accord to the Gulf of Crisa, below Delphi. There the god revealed himself to the astonished passengers of the ship and led them to his temple. Thus these Cretans became the first priests of the oracle.

Apollo was the god of light, and so it was natural that his worship should be closely bound up with prophecy, the art which throws light on the will of the gods. He was, however, also the god of harmony, and thus is also linked with the art of music. At the drinking parties which took place on Olympus he accompanied the Muses on his cithara, while the young goddesses led the dance. Both Leto and Zeus were proud of their son, who was radiant with grace and beauty.

Asteria

A certain myth relates that Zeus wanted at one time to make love to Asteria, sister of Leto. She jumped into the sea to avoid his advances, whereupon Zeus punished her by turning her into a floating island, which was where Leto later took refuge to give birth to Apollo. From that point the island stopped wandering over the seas and took the name of Delos.

The Hyperboreans

The Hyperboreans, who lived at the world's end, spent their days in singing and dancing, and were unacquainted with sickness or old age. Those of them who became sated with the pleasures of the world above put an end to their lives by leaping from a high rock, garlanded and laughing, after a splendid banquet. It was here, in the country of the Hyperboreans, that Apollo lived for the three months of winter when he was not at Delphi.

39

With a laurel wreath on his hair and a sprig of laurel in his hand, Apollo is pursuing a girl, perhaps Daphne. (Red-figure hydria, 450 - 440 BC).

Escapades of Apollo

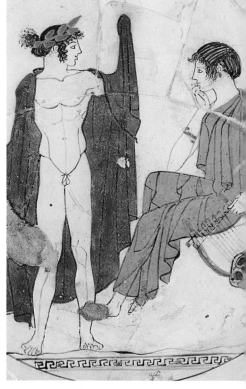

Aristaeus, son of Apollo and Cyrene, was, according to tradition, 'an excellent farmer' and 'a bringer of gifts'. Here he is shown winged, holding a digging tool and his bag of gifts: oil, honey, and milk. (Detail). (Black-figure amphora, c. 540 BC).

A pollos's first love is said to have been Daphne, the daughter of the river Peneus. He fell in love with her one day when he met her alone in the countryside. He instantly wished to make her his own, but she wished to remain chaste and ran away from him. Just as the god was stretching out his arms to take her, Daphne called upon her father and he changed her into a tree - *daphne*, the laurel. Thus the laurel became a tree sacred to Apollo. With laurel leaves he decked his hair and his lyre, while the Pythia, the priestess of Delphi, chewed laurel leaves before delivering oracles.

There was also another daughter of a river, the Euenus, whom Apollo wished to make his wife. She, however, was abducted by Idas, whom Homer describes as the bravest of men dwelling on the earth. Apollo hunted down Idas, and, when he found him, started a wrestling match with him. At this point, Zeus intervened and decreed that the girl, Marpessa, should choose the man she would marry. Marpessa, reflecting that the god would abandon her when she was no longer young, decided to live with Idas. However, Apollo did sleep with many beautiful women. Among them were the Muse Calliope and her sister Thaleia, who gave birth to the Corybantes, young warriors who are identified with the Curetes, who looked after Zeus

Apollo's conflict with Idas for the love of Marpessa is depicted here. The god, between his mother, Leto, and his sister, Artemis, is preparing to hurl his arrow at Idas. (Attic red-figure psychter, c. 480 BC).

Apollo, with a laurel wreath resting on his hair, lifts his garment while he turns his gaze on a nymph or Muse who holds a lyre. (Interior of a kylix with a white background, c. 460 BC).

at his birth. The god also had relations with nymphs and mortal women and had a large number of children, including Amphissus, the eponymous hero of Amphissa, and Chaeron, who built Chaeronea. The beautiful Cyrene, daughter of the King of the Lapiths, Hypseus, gave him a son, Aristaeus, who taught mankind beekeeping and had the gift of delivering them from epidemics.

Of all the sons of Apollo, the most important was the physician Asclepius, who was the fruit of his union with Coronis, daughter of the Thessalian king Phlegyas. When Zeus struck Asclepius with a thunderbolt, Apollo took his revenge by killing Sterope, Bronte, and Arge, the three Cyclopes who made Zeus his thunderbolts. In his anger, Zeus decreed that he should serve a mortal, Admetus, King of Thessaly, for nine years.

The god was punished in a similar way in another instance. The reason this time was that he had taken part in a conspiracy organised by Hera with Athena and Poseidon against Zeus. The conspiracy was a failure, and on the orders of Zeus, Apollo and Poseidon entered the service of Laomedon, King of Troy, and it was the two gods who built the city's mighty walls. However, when they finished, Laomedon refused to give them the agreed fee, so the two deities took a harsh revenge: Poseidon sent floods to Troy and Apollo a plague.

Admetus and Alcestis

Admetus behaved with great respect towards his divine servant, and for that reason Apollo helped him to take for his wife Alcestis, the most beautiful of the daughters of Pelias, King of Iolcus. Moreover, since Apollo knew that Admetus was fated to die very young, he persuaded the Fates to postpone his death, as long as someone else could be found to die in his place. But when the hour came, no one was willing to sacrifice himself for the sake of Admetus, not even his aged parents. The only person to offer herself was Alcestis. As her luck would have it, at the time when Death was taking her, Heracles passed that way and succeeded in rescuing her. Thus Alcestis was returned alive to her husband.

41

Artemis,
goddess of the hunt

Artemis, with a wreath of leaves on her hair and jewellery, wears a pleated tunic, a fawn-skin, and a quiver at her back. She holds a bowl in her left hand, while she tenderly stretches out her right to the swan which stands in front of her. (White lekythos, c. 490 BC).

Artemis, another of the daughters of Zeus (her mother was Leto) was born on Delos on the same day as her brother Apollo. When she was still a child she asked her father that she should remain free of the bonds of marriage. Thus she spent the greater part of her time chasing wild animals on the mountains and in the glens, or protecting their young. For this reason she is called in Homer 'agrotere' - she who wanders in the countryside - 'iocheaira' - shooter of arrows - and 'chryselakatos' - she of the golden bow. For company in her hunts she had the nymphs of the woods and in the dances which took place on Olympus, the Graces. This beautiful goddess was particularly gentle and protective towards innocent youths and unmarried girls. When Pandareus was killed by Zeus for stealing a golden dog, the work of Hephaestus, from the temple of the god in Crete, Artemis, together with Aphrodite and Athena, looked after his orphaned daughters.

At other times, however, Artemis was cruel and relentless. Actaeon, the son of Aristaeus and Autonoe, daughter of Cadmus, who saw her naked as she was bathing in a spring, was severely punished. She changed him into a deer and set his fifty dogs on him to tear him to pieces. Niobe, the wife of Amphion, King of Thebes, also experienced the vengeance of Artemis and Apollo. Proud of her fourteen children, seven sons and seven daughters, she dared to boast that she was better than Leto, who

Here Artemis is shown as the mistress of nature, as the 'Potnia' of the beasts, winged and holding a panther in one hand and a deer in the other. (Detail from the handle.). (Black-figure krater, known as the 'François Vase', c. 570 BC)

had only had two. As soon as Leto's two children learnt of this insult to their mother, they killed twelve of Niobe's children, Apollo the boys and Artemis the girls.

There are many stories of the tricks used by the goddess to avoid her would-be suitors. At one point, the river Alpheus, who was in love with her, planned to take her by surprise during the course of an all-night feast held by Artemis and her friends in his part of the world. But the goddess, suspecting his intentions, took her own measures. She and all the girls in her entourage attended the feast with their faces smeared with clay. Thus Alpheus was unable to tell which of them was Artemis, and so his designs were frustrated.

Artemis discharges her arrows against Actaeon, to punish him for seeing her naked as she bathed in the streams of Cithaeron. (Red-figure krater, c. 470 BC)

The origins of Artemis

Artemis, whose name cannot be derived etymologically from Greek, seems to have come to Greece from Asia Minor. As goddess of the open countryside and of newborn animals, she took the place of an Achaean divinity - the 'Potnia' of the beasts, that is, the mistress of wild animals. Artemis was also identified with Selene (the Moon) and other goddesses of a lunar character such as Rhea, Cybele, and Hecate, and was the female equivalent of Apollo, the sun god. In addition, Artemis protected childbirth and, in a wider sense, motherhood and the upbringing of children.

Only once did the indomitable daughter of Zeus fail to emerge victorious. In the Trojan War, Artemis, who supported the Trojans, in her full armour, found herself face to face with Hera, who took the side of the Greeks. In her anger, Hera threw far away, with one hand, her adversary's bow and quiver and forced her, the dauntless Artemis, to run away with tears in her eyes.

The theft of the cattle of Apollo by the new-born Hermes is the subject of this picture. The cattle are hidden in a cave on the left, while Hermes is shown in another cave, on the right, lying in a cradle and pretending to know nothing. Apollo has come to complain to the thief's parents, Zeus and Maia.(Caeretan hydria, c. 520 BC).

Hermes,
messenger of the gods

Here Hermes is shown carrying out a command of Zeus: to bring the new-born Dionysus to the nymphs for them to bring him up. In the other hand he probably held a bunch of grapes, which the infant god is trying to reach. (Statue of Hermes by Praxiteles, c. 330 BC).

F rom the very first day of his life Hermes showed himself worthy of his title of patron of thieves. His parents were Zeus and the blushful Maia, daughter of Atlas. He was born in the cave where his mother lived, and she, as soon as he was born, swaddled him and went about her business. This was the chance which the cunning infant god had been waiting for. Unhesitatingly, he jumped from his cradle and went out into the yard. Finding a tortoise there, he killed it and made out of its shell the world's first lyre.

Later, when he tired of playing the lyre, he went and stole fifty cows from Apollo's herd. So that the theft should not be discovered, he made the cows walk backwards, so that their footprints showed them going in the opposite direction to the route which they actually followed. He himself left no footprints at all, because he bound tamarisk and myrtle twigs on to his feet. The only person to see him on the way was an old man, whose silence Hermes attempted to purchase with promises. When he reached Pylos, he slaughtered two of the cows to eat, hid the rest, and returned to his cradle as if nothing had happened. In the meantime, Apollo, who had obtained information from the old man, realised that the thief was his new-born half-brother. He immediately set out to find him, but got nowhere with him, since Hermes played the part of the innocent infant. So he dragged him to Olympus, to appear before their father, Zeus. He, having heard the charming lies of his youngest son, decided that the two brothers should be reconciled. Thus Hermes was

Hermes, as Psychopompus ('guide of souls'), leads a young woman, Myrrhine, by the hand to the Acheron river; from there Charon will convey her to the country of the dead. On the left her relatives are shown bidding her farewell. (Marble lekythos, 430 - 420 BC).

Hermes, carrying out the orders of Zeus, with the 'hat of darkness' and his winged sandals, holds in his left hand a wine cup (kantharos) together with his wand, and in his right a wine-pourer. The Satyr is playing the stringed barbiton, whose melodies have captivated the deer which accompanies them. (Red-figure amphora, 500 - 490 BC).

forced to take Apollo to the place where he had hidden the animals. There, to win him over, he gave him his lyre. Apollo, delighted by its sound - never heard before - accepted the gift and gave Hermes in exchange a shepherd's crook, thus appointing him their protector.

When Hermes grew up, he became the messenger of the gods. With wings on his back, sandals, wearing his winged hat - the petasos - and holding his golden rod, the caduceus - so that everyone would know that he was the official emissary of Zeus, he conveyed the latter's commands to gods and men. His quick-wittedness and diplomacy enabled him to accomplish even the most difficult missions. In addition, as Hermes Psychopompus, he conducted the souls of the dead to Hades. The ancients believed that he was the first student of astronomy, and for this reason gave his name to one of the planets. He was also regarded as the god of luck, and so anything found by chance was seen as a gift from Hermes and was called a 'hermaion'. The character of Hermes is also apparent in his love affairs. Most of his erotic desires were fulfilled by trickery - and he bequeathed his cunning to his descendants, a typical example of whom is Autolycus, the grandfather of the wily Odysseus.

The origins of Hermes

Hermes is a very ancient divinity and one with a genuine Greek - and folk - pedigree. His characteristics and the properties attributed to him place him in the category of the wind gods.

Iris

Iris, the winged daughter of Thaumas, son of Pontus, and of the Oceanid Electra, herself initially performed the duties of a messenger. The appearance on the scene of Hermes, however, limited her activities. The ancients believed that the gods used Iris for missions to women and Hermes for those to men, or that Iris was exclusively the messenger of Hera and Hermes of Zeus.

Bronze statuette of Hermes bearing a ram, from Sparta, c. 500 BC.

Ares, god of war

Ares, the harsh and relentless god of war, was one of the children of Hera and Zeus. Because of his unstable and lawless character, this god was not much liked either among the gods or among men. The places where he was worshipped were few, and no city invoked him as its protector. Unlike his sister Athena, who combined valour in war with prudence, Ares represented the unreasoning frenzy of war and for that reason took pleasure in slaughter and bloodshed.

His inseparable companions in battle were his two sons by Aphrodite, Deimos and Phobos, who personify terror and flight in the face of the enemy. The beautiful Aphrodite presented Ares with two other children, Harmonia and Eros. This god was also regarded as the father of bloodthirsty kings such as Oenomaus, King of Olympia, and Diomedes, King of Thrace and owner of the famous man-eating horses. Penthesilea, Queen of the Amazons, who hastened to the assistance of the Trojans after the death of Hector, was also his daughter.

The relationship between Ares and Aphrodite was irregular, since she was married to Hephaestus. But Hephaestus was lame, while Ares was young and handsome. Furthermore, Aphrodite had not chosen marriage with Hephaestus of her own free will: it had

Ares, fully armed, sits next to the fair Aphrodite Detail from a gathering of the gods. (Red-figure kylix, c. 520 BC).

The two lovers Ares and Aphrodite have been surprised by the presence of Helios (the Sun), while their guard Alectryon has fallen asleep. This wall-painting is derived from an original of the early Hellenistic period. (Wall-painting from Pompeii, c. 10 BC).

Ares, the cruel god of war, is shown fully armed in this detail. (Black-figure krater, known as the 'François Vase', c. 570 BC).

been forced upon her by Hera. Thus, whenever Hephaestus was away, Aphrodite secretly entertained the god of war in her husband's palace. But Helios (the Sun), who sees all things, told Hephaestus everything. Hephaestus thereupon constructed metal netting, as fine as a spider's web and invisible to the naked eye, and draped it all over his marriage bed. He then told his wife that he had business to do on Lemnos, and left. Ares had no intention of losing such a fine opportunity and hastened to the embrace of Aphrodite. But as soon as they got into bed, they found themselves entangled in the nets and unable to move. In the meantime, Hephaestus, again with Helios as his informant, returned to the palace and summoned all the gods with his shouting (the goddesses were too modest to witness such a spectacle). When they saw the two guilty parties tied naked to the bed, they burst out laughing, and Apollo, turning to Hermes, asked him if he would mind being in Ares' place, to which he replied, laughing, that he would not mind being in bed with Aphrodite, even if he was tied down by three time as many bonds. Finally, the two deities were set free, thanks to the mediation of Poseidon. Aphrodite left in haste for Paphos in Cyprus, where the Graces were waiting to bathe and dress her, while Ares took refuge in the land of the warlike Thracians, where he delighted in spending his time.

The Areopagus

According to the local traditions of Athens, Ares saw one of his daughters, Alcippe, being raped by Halirrhothius, a son of Poseidon, and in his anger killed him. Poseidon, embittered by the death of his son, called upon the other gods to try the murderer. The trial took place on a rock at Athens, and the accused was found not guilty. It was from Ares, the first accused, that the Areopagus (*pagos* = rock), the court which tried murder charges at Athens, took its name.

47

Aphrodite, goddess of beauty and of love

*A*ccounts of the birth of Aphrodite differ. Some said that she was generated by the white foam which formed when Cronus threw the genitals of Uranus into the sea, while others maintained that she was the daughter of Zeus and Dione. Everyone, however, honoured and revered this most beautiful of goddesses. It was her power which spread sexual attraction not only among mortals, but also among the gods.

Although she was married to Hephaestus, Aphrodite was free with her favours to Ares and to other gods. As a result of her relations with Poseidon, she brought into the world Eryx, King of Sicily, while it was said that Rhodos (Rhodes) was their daughter. Aphrodite also fell in love with Dionysus and, without loss of time, slept with him. At some point, however, when the god was far away in India, she had an affair with a youth renowned for his beauty, Adonis. When Dionysus returned, Aphrodite was already pregnant, either by him or by Adonis. Hera, in her hatred for Dionysus and Aphrodite, who were the bastard children of her husband, made her give birth to a boy of great ugliness, Priapus. This shameless god of fertility, when he grew up, joined the entourage of Dionysus.

Just like the rest of the gods, Aphrodite used her power sometimes for good and sometimes for evil purposes. Thus, those who scorned her were severely punished. Eos, the goddess of the dawn, who once slept with Ares, was condemned constantly to seek fresh

The birth of Aphrodite. (Relief, c. 465 BC).

The goat-footed Pan attempts to embrace the naked Aphrodite, while she lifts her sandal to him to frighten him off. (Aphrodite-Pan group, c. 100 BC).

Aphrodite is shown conversing with Eros in this detail, together with Eunomia and Paedia - personifications of abstract concepts. (Red-figure lekythos, c. 410 BC).

lovers. She took vengeance upon Tyndareus, King of Sparta, who had failed to honour her as she should, by making his daughters, Helen and Clytemnestra, gain a bad reputation for their infidelity to their husbands.

On the other hand, she released Selemnus, a handsome youth who had fallen in love with the nymph Argyra, but had been deserted by her, from his torments by changing him into a river. But even as a river, Selemnus continued to love Argyra, so the goddess granted him oblivion, and from then on those who bathed in the waters of Selemnus were cured of all their erotic passions.

One of Aphrodite's favourite amusements was to make her father, Zeus, descend to the earth and sleep with mortal women, with the result that he had to contend with the anger of Hera. When this became too much to stand, Zeus paid her back in her own coin. He awoke in her heart a passion for a mortal man, the handsome Anchises of Troy. The goddess, disguised as a mortal, succeeded in sleeping with Anchises and, some months later, became the mother of Aeneas, one of the greatest heroes of the Trojan War.

Eros

Aphrodite was always attended by a large retinue of girl friends and helpers, such as Hebe, Harmonia, the Graces, the Hours, and Peitho, the goddess who persuaded girls to surrender to love. However, the god who was almost always at her side was her son Eros. Men imagined him as a boy with golden wings on his back and with a bow in his hands. With his magical arrows, which he fired into the hearts of mortals and immortals, he brought lovers together. With the passage of time, in poetry and the visual arts, many Erotes ('cupids') made their appearance in the place of the one.

49

Hephaestus,
god of metalwork

In this detail, Hephaestus, as the wonderful blacksmith that he was, with his tongs in his hand and his hammer on his shoulder, returns to Olympus accompanied by Dionysus, on his right. As he is half-drunk, he is supported by a Satyr. (Red-figure pelike, 435 - 430 BC).

*T*he only one of the Olympian gods to have some physical defect was Hephaestus, the son of Zeus and Hera. He was born lame, and his mother, ashamed of him, threw him into the sea to drown. But he had the good fortune to be taken into the protection of two sea goddesses, the Nereid Thetis and the Oceanid Eurynome. Thus the god spent his childhood in the cave of Nereus, making women's jewellery.

However, the time came when he grew tired of living in the depths of the sea, so he resolved that not only would he be accepted on Olympus, but also that he would take vengeance on his mother. For this purpose, he fashioned a splendid throne of gold, winding invisible nets around it, and sent it as a gift to Hera. She gladly accepted the offering of her son, but as soon as she sat on it, she found herself trapped in the nets. After much deliberation among the gods and an unsuccessful attempt on the part of Ares to talk to Hephaestus, the matter was taken in hand by Dionysus. He went and found his brother, got him drunk, and led him in triumph to Olympus. In the heavens Hephaestus was reconciled to his mother and she, in order to appease him, gave him Aphrodite as his wife. There is, however, another version of the story which says that he married Aglaïa, the youngest of the three Graces.

Some also said that the god was not a cripple from birth, but that once when Zeus was having one of his usual quarrels with Hera, Hephaestus hastened to defend his mother, whereupon Zeus seized him by the leg and threw him down to earth. He fell for a whole day and finally landed on Lemnos, where he was looked after by the Sintians, the inhab-

One day, Zeus and Hera had a mighty quarrel on Olympus, and Hephaestus hastened to defend his mother. But Zeus managed to throw him from the threshold of Olympus. This scene, shown here, is watched in amazement by a female sea deity on the right and Athena Promachos, standing on a rock, on the left. (Architectural frieze, after 150 AD).

Thetis receives from Hephaestus the weapons of her son Achilles, forged by the hand of the god. (Interior of a red-figure kylix, c. 480 BC).

itants of the island. It was in this way that he became lame, while Lemnos was his favourite island and it was there that he set up his workshop.

Hephaestus was a god of many talents. He was a builder and architect, a goldsmith and an armourer, a worker in bronze and the inventor of mechanical devices. It was Hephaestus who built the magnificent palaces of the gods on Olympus. He also made two girls of gold to support himself on, since his legs were weak. He is also said to have fashioned a bronze giant, Talus, whom he gave to Minos, King of Crete. Talus used to walk around Crete three times a day and burnt any enemy he caught by pressing him against his red-hot bronze chest. For Alcinous, King of the Phaeacians he made immortal dogs of silver and gold to guard the gates of his palace. To show his gratitude to Helios, who had helped him during the Battle of the Giants, he filled the palace of his son, Aeetes, at Colchis, with superb pieces of his workmanship. Of these the most noteworthy were four magic fountains which ran with milk, wine, perfume, and water (hot or cold, depending upon the season of the year). Of the many other wonderful objects which were the work of his hands, the most famous were the weapons of the two great heroes Heracles and Achilles.

The cult of Hephaestus

Hephaestus was the god who represented fire. The ancient inhabitants of Lemnos believed that the volcanic fires which sprang from the Mosychlus mountain came from the underground workshop of the god. Around the end of the 6th century, the cult spread from Lemnos to Athens, where Hephaestus became the patron of workers in bronze, together with Athena. In the 5th century BC, the Athenians built a fine temple in the Agora - now erroneously called the Theseion - to honour these two divinities.

51

Dionysus,
god of wine

Dionysus, in ecstasy, plays the barbiton. Two Satyrs dance around him with castanets.
(Interior of a red-figure kylix, c. 480 BC).

One day, Zeus was gazing at the earth from on high when he spied the beautiful Semele, one of the daughters of Cadmus, King of Thebes, and fell in love with her. In order to satisfy his desire for her, he secretly entered the palace of her father one night and slept with her. Hera, however, found out about his infidelity and decided to have her revenge. As she knew that Zeus had promised Semele that he would fulfil any wish she made, she advised the girl to ask that Zeus would appear before her as he had before Hera on the day of their marriage.

Zeus attempted to dissuade her - but in vain. Semele insisted that he should keep his word. So the god appeared before her in his chariot, amid thunder and lightning. The palace was wrapped in flames, and Semele perished - either from terror or struck by lightning. Zeus then took the infant who was already growing inside her and put it in an opening in his thigh. A few months later, Dionysus was born from the thigh of Zeus.

In order to rescue the child from the wrath of Hera, Zeus entrusted him initially to Ino, the sister of Semele; afterwards he gave him to the nymphs who lived on a mountain in Asia Minor, Nyssa, for them to bring him up. In spite of this, when Dionysus grew up, Hera succeeded in driving him mad. After wandering in Egypt and Syria, the god came to Phrygia, where he was cured by Rhea. He then journeyed to Greece in order to spread his worship among the people there and to teach them how to cultivate the vine.

Wearing an ivy wreath, Dionysus, with the thyrsos in one hand and a drum in the other, sits on the back of the animal sacred to him, the panther. (Mosaic floor from the 'House of the Masks' on Delos, second half of the 2nd century BC.).

Maenads in a state of ecstasy (detail). (Attic red-figure stamnos, c. 420 BC).

Small bronze head of Dionysus, wreathed with ivy. (Bronze statuette of Dionysus from Acarnania, 2nd century BC).

The cult of Dionysus

Dionysus was a god of wine and, more generally, of fertility and vegetation. The chief characteristic of the cult was ecstasy, that is, the transcending of the normal self thanks to the use of wine and of frenzied dancing. Various rites were performed in honour of Dionysus. In the orgies - which means 'sacred works' and which were held every two years on Mt Parnassus - only women, the Maenads or Bacchae, took part, worshipping the god in the manner of the Maenads of myth. They would fall into a state of religious hysteria and run about the mountains, where they saw rivers of honey, milk, and wine springing from the earth, and would tear apart with their bare hands any wild animal they came across. Similar orgiastic rites were held in other parts of Greece.

On his journeys, Dionysus did not travel alone. His constant companions were the nymphs of Nyssa who had brought him up, and Sileni, Satyrs, Maenads, and Pan, a jolly, lustful god with horns and the legs of a goat. The Sileni were men with animal faces, a horse's tail and a horse's legs. Their favourite occupations were drinking, singing, and chasing nymphs. The Satyrs greatly resembled the Sileni: so much so that some maintained that Sileni and Satyrs were two different names for the same horse-like demons of the woods. The Maenads were women who entered a state of ecstasy and worshipped the god in a frenzied manner. They are often shown in vase paintings dancing in an abandoned way and holding the 'thyrsos', a rod crowned with ivy or with a pine cone on the end. In many scenes they are holding animals which they have caught in their wanderings in the woods and on the mountains, or are tearing apart small deer.

The wife of Dionysus was Ariadne, the daughter of Minos. He found her on Naxos, where Theseus had abandoned her, and fell in love with her. Staphylus and Oenopion were sons of Dionysus and Ariadne.

Asclepius, god of medicine

At Laceria, a city in Thessaly, Phlegyas, the son of Ares, once ruled as king. This king had a beautiful daughter, Coronis, whom Apollo chanced to see one day and, falling in love with her, made her his own. The girl was ashamed of her encounter with the great god and told no one of it; besides, she was already engaged to Ischys, the son of the King of Arcadia. On the day of their wedding, a crow, seeing the preparations which were being made, flew to Delphi to inform the god that his beloved was marrying a mortal. Apollo flew into a rage with the crow which had been in such a hurry to bring him the bad news and cursed it - and the crow, originally white, turned black. Then Apollo killed Ischys with his arrows, while his sister Artemis slew Coronis and the women of her entourage.

However, Coronis was pregnant and Apollo did not wish the child to be lost. So, a little before the girl's body was burned on the funeral pyre, he snatched the infant - Asclepius - and took him to Pelion, where he entrusted him to the Centaur Chiron. From this wise Centaur Asclepius learnt, among many other things, how to heal every sickness and every wound. Such was his skill as a physician that his

Hygeia, one of the daughters of Asclepius. The others were Iaso, Aceso, and Panacea. (Head of a statue of the goddess Hygeia, c. 360 BC).

name rapidly became known throughout Greece and a host of the sick and wounded flocked to him to be cured. When, however, Asclepius went so far as to raise the dead, he provoked the wrath of Zeus. The god aimed a thunderbolt at the son of Apollo and struck him dead.

According to one myth, Asclepius had the power to raise the dead because he had shared with Athena the blood which had flowed when Perseus cut off the head of the Gorgon. This blood had a double power: it could either save people or wipe them out. The Greeks honoured Asclepius initially as a hero and later, from the late Classical period onwards, as a god. His wife was said to have been Epione, a figure without a history whose name is simply derived from his own. His daughters by Epione, Hygeia, Iaso, Aceso, and Panacea are personifications of abstract concepts connected with medicine.

The Centaur Chiron

The Centaurs were creatures which were men from the waist up and horses from the waist down, living in the woods and on the mountains. Most of them were violent, as unrestrainable as natural forces, always liable to make trouble and to quarrel. Chiron, however, resembled them only in his outer form. He was calm, just, wise, and fond of human beings, and undertook the upbringing of those children who were entrusted to him. Many generations of heroes who later became renowned for their exploits were taught by him. The good Centaur was once accidentally wounded by Heracles. As he was in terrible pain, but could not go to his rest because he was immortal, he asked Prometheus to exchange his life for his own immortality. Thus Prometheus became immortal and Chiron found peace in death.

There are also references to two sons of Asclepius, Machaon and Podalirius, who took part in the campaign against Troy as warriors and physicians.

Gods of the Underworld

Pluto and Persephone were rulers of the Underworld. In this picture they sit on their throne with the gravity of sacred figures. Pluto holds a bowl and flowers, Persephone a cockerel and ears of corn. (Locri tablet, 470 - 460 BC).

*T*he absolute ruler of the Underworld was Pluto or Hades, like Zeus and Poseidon, a son of Cronus. Pluto was, however, not only a god of death: people believed that it was through his mediation that the earth yielded them its fruits. Thus he was honoured as a god of fertility and of wealth.

The wife of Pluto, Persephone, was also regarded as a goddess of the dead and of the life-giving earth. After her abduction by the god and the agreement reached by her mother, Demeter, with Pluto, Persephone spent eight months of the year above the earth and the rest with her husband. When she was in the world above, the earth turned green and prepared to bring forth its fruits. It was in summer that she descended to the kingdom of Hades, at the time when the sun was scorching the earth and the fields lay fallow.

The Underworld, the melancholy place where the souls of the dead were gathered together, was also called Hades. It was a large enclosed area beneath the earth, the gate of which was guarded by the dog Cerberus, who allowed entry, but not departure. Only certain great heroes, such as Heracles and Odysseus, were able to visit the Underworld and return alive to earth.

Initially, the Greeks believed that it was Hermes who led the souls of the dead to the gate of Hades. Later, another deity of the Underworld, Charon, made his appearance. At many periods the belief prevailed that Charon took the souls in his

Charon was a demonic figure of the Underworld, charged with bringing souls from the world of the living to the world of the dead. In the picture Charon, in his boat, is listening carefully to Hermes Psychopompus, who has come to hand over a dead woman (not included in the picture). (White lekythos, 450 BC).

Hades-Pluto, as a chthonic deity, was not only god of death, but also of fertility and wealth. Here he is shown reclining on the same couch as his wife, Persephone, holding a bowl in one hand and a horn of plenty in the other. (Interior of a red-figure kylix, c. 440 BC).

boat to the Underworld, crossing the waters of the Acherousia lake or the River Acheron. The name Charon means 'causer of joy' and was obviously given to the god as a euphemism. When the dead reached Hades, they presented themselves before its three judges: Minos, Rhadamanthus, and Aeacus. Minos, whose laws established while he lived remained etched on the memory of man for thousands of years, and Rhadamanthus, who was able to judge disputes between men and impose the implementation of the law, were sons of Zeus and Europa. Aeacus, the wise and just King of Aegina, was a son of Zeus and the nymph Aegina, daughter of the river god Asopus. It is said that Rhadamanthus judged the souls of Asians and Aeacus those of Europeans, while Minos, whose authority was superior to that of the other two, decided disputed cases.

The torments of Sisyphus and Tantalus

In the kingdom of Hades, punishments for sinners were harsh. Sisyphus, king of Corinth, who had shown irreverence towards Zeus and the gods of the Underworld, was condemned to push a huge rock up a steep slope; but as soon as it reached the top, the rock rolled back to the bottom, thus perpetuating his torment. The king Tantalus, who dared to reveal divine secrets to mortals and slaughtered his own son to offer him as a banquet to the gods, had been sentenced to eternal hunger and thirst. As soon as he bent to take a drink of water, it would disappear, and as soon as he stretched out his hand to pluck some fruit, a strong wind would blow the trees out of his reach.

The rising sun (Helios).
(Metope of the Temple of Athena at Ilium, early
3rd century BC).

Lesser gods

The Nereids, fifty sea goddesses, lived in the depths of the sea with their father, the aged Nereus, dancing, singing, and playing in the waves. In this vase-painting, while Heracles wrestles with Triton, son of their sister Amphitrite, they have started to dance, as carefree as the waves. (Interior of a black-figure kylix, c. 550 BC).

A part from the gods who have already been described, the imagination of the Greeks fashioned a whole host of other divine figures. One of these was Helios (the Sun), the son of the Titan Hyperion. Driving his fiery chariot with its winged horses, with his abundant golden hair streaming behind him, Helios made his daily morning journey from East to West. In the evening, the god was conveyed in a golden goblet back to his starting-point. The sisters of Helios were Selene (the Moon), whose name means 'bright and shining', and 'rosy-fingered' Eos, the personification of dawn. The stars were also given human form, while Iris, the divine messenger, represented the rainbow.

A goddess who was very powerful before the twelve gods of Olympus took the rule over the world into their hands was Hecate, daughter of Perses, the son of the Titan Creius. Another account says that Hecate was the daughter of Zeus and that Zeus honoured her as he did few other goddesses.

Among the deities of the earth, together with Ge, Rhea, the goat-footed Pan, and Priapus, was a goddess of Phrygian origin, Cybele. She was regarded as a goddess of vegetation and fertility and as the ruler of wild beasts. Her worship took place on mountains with wild cries, ecstatic dances, and the music of pipes, drums, cymbals, and castanets.

Another category of deities were those who appear in groups, such as the Muses, the Sirens, the Fates, the Furies, the Hours, the Graces, the Hesperides, the Sileni, the Satyrs, the Curetes, the Corybantes, the Giants, the Gorgons, the Harpies, and the Winds. Also in this category are the nymphs, god-

Eos (dawn) and Helios (the Sun), with nimbuses, ride in their chariots. The winged youth holding the reins must be Phosphorus, the star which shines in the sky at dawn.
(Apulian krater, late 4th century BC).

The Muses, the nine daughters of Zeus, led the dance with songs and music on Olympus, at Pieria, and on Parnassus and Helicon, extolling the greatness of their father. In this picture, one of the Muses plays her cithara on Mt Helicon. Before her is a nightingale, the Muses' favourite bird.
(White lekythos, c. 440 BC).

Cybele was originally a Phrygian goddess of the earth, vegetation, and fertility, ruler of the mountains and of wild beasts. Here she is shown with her beloved, the beautiful Attis, holding a rod in one hand and a drum in the other. By her side is the animal sacred to her, the lion.
(Votive relief, c. 230 BC).

desses of vegetation who lived on the mountains, in the woods, and in rivers and springs. They were the companions of other gods, such as Pan and Dionysus, fell in love with gods or mortals and, often, undertook the upbringing of gods and heroes. The Nereids, the fifty enchanting daughters of Nereus, were also divinities who belonged to a group. They lived in a silver cave in the depths of the sea. From there they always set out readily to help gods, heroes, and mortals, to calm tempests, and to help sailors.

Of the rest of the gods, the following minor deities can be briefly mentioned: Tyche, the personification of the abstract notion of chance; Ate, whose name means 'disaster' and who was a daughter of Eris; the Litae, daughters of Zeus, who hastened to make good the evils caused by Ate; Hubris, the personification of man's presumptuous behaviour, and two sons of Night: Hypnos, the young and beautiful god of sleep, and Thanatos (Death), who carried off with him for ever any mortal man he met.

Mythical places and peoples

The Greeks believed in the existence of various mythical places, such as the country of the Hyperboreans and the Islands of the Blest. The Islands of the Blest are probably to be identified with the Elysian Fields, a paradisal place inhabited by heroes to whom the gods had granted immortality.

Mythical peoples included the gigantic, one-eyed Cyclopes, who were divided into three races: the man-eaters, whom Odysseus met on his way back to Ithaca, the thunderbolt-makers, who fashioned these weapons for Zeus and the 'gastrocheires' ('belly-builders'), who were good builders and were so-called because they filled their bellies by the labour of their hands. The gigantic walls of Tiryns, Argos, and Mycenae were regarded as the work of these Cyclopes and were thus called 'Cyclopean walls'.

With a snake instead of a band in her hair and holding a thyrsus in her left hand and a leopard in her right, a Maenad dances in ecstasy. (Interior of a kylix with white background, 490 - 485 BC).

Dionysus with dancing Maenads. (Attic black-figure amphora, signed by the potter Amasis and attributed to the Amasis Painter, 540 - 530 BC).

THE HEROES
The heroes
THE HEROES

THE HEROES

*T*he gods were not the only protagonists in the Greek myths: there were also certain exceptional mortals, gifted with beauty and intelligence, with courage and magnanimity - in other words, the heroes. The heroes were those who rid the world of monsters, wiped out bloodthirsty robbers, and redressed injustices of every kind.

Although today the word 'hero' is generally taken to mean one who is brave and courageous in war, in antiquity it was a broader expression of honour and respect. In Homer's epics the Iliad and the Odyssey, it is first and foremost kings and nobles who are described as 'heroes'; these are followed by those who take part in a war, and then by those who stand out for some quality, such as Demodocus in his art as a bard and Mulius in his art as a herald. Since, however, the most highly-regarded virtue among the characters of Homer was courage, the word 'hero' soon came to mean the brave warrior.

The heroes of myth were usually of divine birth. They also enjoyed divine protection: in tight corners in their lives, some god frequently made his appearance to help, protect, and advise. This does not mean that the heroes did not take their own

The Amazon Antiope fell in love with Theseus when the hero was taking part in the campaign of Heracles in the country of the Amazons in Pontus. On his return, Theseus took the Amazon with him to Greece. Here, Theseus is abducting Antiope.
(Group of Theseus and Antiope from the Battle of the Amazons on the western pediment of the Temple of Daphnephoros Apollo at Eretria, c. 510 BC).

initiatives. Odysseus, on his return journey to Ithaca, had the support of Athena, Hermes, and other deities. But in most cases it was his own cleverness and prudence which saved him. Achilles, though under the guardianship of Athena and of his mother, Thetis, resolved to take vengeance for the death of his beloved friend, Patroclus, even though he knew that this would mean his own end.

An important role was also played in the lives of the heroes by oracles and seers. They resorted to oracles, such as that of Apollo at Delphi, or of Zeus at Dodona, to learn the will of the gods, to receive replies to questions which concerned them or to discover what fate had in store for them. At the oracle of Apollo, the priestess, called the Pythia, chewed laurel leaves before speaking as from the mouth of the god. At the oracle of Zeus, the pronouncements were made by priests who first listened to the rustling of the sacred oak which grew in the holy precinct. Of the seers of myth, the most famous were Calchas, who accompanied the Achaeans on the campaign against Troy, and Tiresias, who, though blind, saw the truth.

Heracles, wearing a helmet which is in the shape of a lion's head in front, fires his bow at a Trojan warrior. (From the eastern pediment of the Temple of Aphaea on Aegina, c. 490 BC).

Heracles

An imposing depiction of Heracles. He is holding the tripod which he stole from the sanctuary of Delphi, while his head emerges from the open mouth of the lion skin which he wears on his shoulders; he is holding his club, and his sword hangs on his left side. (Red-figure vase of the early 5th century BC).

*A*t the time when one of the sons of Perseus, Electryon, ruled at Mycenae, the Taphii, des-cendants of his brother Mestor, who up till then had lived on the Echinades is-lands, arrived there to lay claim to the lands of their father. However, Electryon refused to recognise their rights. In the conflict which followed, all nine sons of the king lost their lives, while those of the invaders who survived returned whence they had come. At that point, Electryon decided to entrust the rule and his only daughter, Alcmene, to his wife's brother Amphitryon, and to start a war against the Taphii. As bad luck would have it, Amphitryon became the involun-tary cause of Electryon's death, a little before he planned to embark upon his cam-paign. This was the opportunity which Sthenelus, another brother of Amphitryon, had been waiting for. He took the rule into his own hands and drove out Amphi-tryon and his supporters from Mycenae. Alcmene, who followed Amphitryon, promised that she would be his wife if he avenged the death of her brothers. The exiles finally found shelter at Thebes, where, with the support of the King, Creon, Amphitryon gathered an army and set out for the islands of the Taphii.

In the meantime, Alcmene, like many other mortal women, caught the eye of Zeus with her beauty. This time, however, the king of the gods did not wish mere-ly to satisfy his erotic desires with her: he wanted to father on her the strongest and most courageous of mortals, capable of ridding mankind of many ills. Thus, one night, he came to her in the guise of Amphitryon and made her his own. A little later, Amphitryon, who had been victorious in the war, returned and slept with her. The outcome of this night's doings made themselves apparent a few

Amphitryon, assisted by Antenor, lights the pyre to burn his unfaithful wife, Alcmene, who, during his absence, had slept with Zeus. Zeus, hearing the pleas of Alcmene, has sent clouds - in the form of girls - to put out the flames. Eos, on the upper right, watches the scene. The rainbow can be seen behind Alcmene. The white dots probably represent the rain storm, or the golden rain which fell from heaven during the union of the god with the mortal. (Paestum krater, 350 - 325 BC).

months later: Alcmene brought twins into the world - Heracles from her union with Zeus, and Iphicles, the son of Amphitryon. When the day came for the birth of Heracles, Zeus called together the other gods and boasted that the child who saw the light that day would rule over the rest of mankind, as he was descended from himself. But Hera resolved to spoil his plans, and made him swear that his words would come true. In order for her plan to succeed, however, another child would

The milk of Hera

Since it was decreed that no son of Zeus could claim divine honours unless he had drunk the milk of Hera, when Heracles was born, Hermes took him and placed him at the breast of the goddess without her realising this. When she saw the trick which Hermes had played - too late, because Heracles had already fed - Hera pulled herself free abruptly and her milk spilled on to the heavens. That, they say, was how the Milky Way was formed.

have to be born that day before Heracles, so she commanded Eileithyia, the goddess of birth, to delay the labour of Alcmene and to bring into the world, very prematurely, Eurystheus, son of Sthenelus and Nicippe. In accordance with the oath of Zeus, Eurystheus would become king, while Heracles, who was born after him, would be forced to serve him.

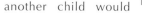

Alcmene, after giving birth to Heracles, decided to abandon the infant in a grove, fearing the jealousy of Hera. But Athena happened to pass that way, accompanied by Hera, who saw the child and admired it. Athena persuaded Hera to feed it at her breast. In the picture, we have a depiction of this moment. Athena, on the left, offers a lily. On the right is the winged Iris.
(Apulian lekythos, 375 - 350 BC).

65

The early years of Heracles

Heracles strangles the two snakes which Hera has sent to his bed to kill him. Athena, on the left, holds a spear in her right hand, while she stretches out her left towards the young Heracles in a gesture of protection. Iphicles, brother of Heracles, stretches out his hands in terror towards his nurse, who rushes to snatch him from the bed. (Red-figure stamnos, c. 480 BC).

*T*he jealousy which Hera felt towards Heracles, her husband's bastard son, was not satisfied by ensuring that he would become the servant of Eurystheus, so she thought up a fearful method of disposing of him. One evening when Heracles and Iphicles were sleeping peacefully in their cradles, she sent two huge serpents to devour the infants. As soon as he saw them, Iphicles began to cry in terror, but Heracles showed no fear at all. He seized the snakes by the throat, strangled them, and threw them at the feet of Amphitryon, who had arrived in the meantime, accompanied by Alcmene and his servants. Then all of them realised that the child was endowed with superhuman strength and worth, and that he was truly a son of Zeus.

As Heracles grew up, he studied at the feet of the most renowned teachers of Greece. He was taught reading, writing, and the cithara by Linus, son of Apollo, who paid dearly for the irascible character of his pupil. One day, Heracles, annoyed by the rebukes of Linus, hit him on the head with the cithara and killed

Heracles, among his fellow-pupils who are strongly complaining, raises a broken stool to threaten his teacher Linus for correcting him during a lesson. (Red-figure kylix, 470 - 460 BC).

him. However, a law of Rhadamanthus, son of Zeus and Europa, laid down that the person who killed someone who had been first to start the quarrel was not regarded as a criminal, and so Heracles was not charged with the murder of Linus. After this, Amphitryon sent the child into the countryside to guard his herds. Heracles was scarely eighteen years old when the opportunity arose for his first great feat. In the region of Mt Cithaeron a terrible lion which decimated the herds of Amphitryon and his neighbour Thespius, King of Thespiae, made its appearance.

Heracles resolved to rid the country of this plague. For the fifty days that he was hunting the lion, the hero was a guest in the palace of Thespius. This king had fifty daughters and wanted all of them to have a child by Heracles. So every night he sent a different daughter to his bed. Heracles, thinking that it was the same one who came each time, slept with all of them, except for one, who resisted. In spite of this, fifty children were born in due course, since one of the girls had twins. As soon as the hero had killed the lion, he left Thespius and his daughters and took the road to Thebes.

The etymology of the name 'Heracles'

According to one account, the hero, who was originally called Alcides, took the name Heracles because, by reason of Hera, whose jealously urged him on to ever more achievements, he acquired *kleos* (= renown). This etymology is today generally accepted, since Heracles belongs to the circle of figures associated with Hera. Another account says that this name was given to him by the Pythia, the priestess of Apollo, when he went to seek an oracle. The reason why the Pythia named him Heracles was that he would gain *kleos aphthiton* (endless glory) by bringing *hera* (benefit) to mankind.

'Heracles Furens'

Hera, with her undying hatred of Heracles, once afflicted him with madness, so that he lost his reason and was seized with a mania for murder and destruction. Here, at the entrance to some monumental building, Heracles in his fury has snatched up a child which he is throwing into the fire together with the objects which he has demolished in his madness. His wife, Megara, tearing her hair, runs off to the right to escape. Over the portico, his nephew Iolaus and Alcmene can be seen in a state of alarm. (Paestum krater, 350 - 325 BC).

On his return from hunting the lion of Cithaeron, Heracles encountered emissaries from Orchomenus who were coming to collect the tribute which Thebes had to pay to their city. The reason for this was that once upon a time the charioteer of Menoeceus, the father of Creon, had fatally injured Clymenus, King of Orchomenus. A little before he died, this king, with his curse, had laid a duty upon his son, Erginus, to avenge his death. And so Erginus fought against the Thebans, conquered them, and forced them to send him a hundred head of cattle each year for twenty years.

As soon as he heard this story, Heracles became furious. He seized the messengers from Orchomenus, cut off their noses and ears, and sent them back home with their hands tied behind their backs, with a message to Erginus that this was the tribute which Thebes paid to Orchomenus. The humiliation for Orchomenus and its king was great, and he decided to declare war on Thebes again. This time, however, Thebes had Heracles as its commander-in-chief. Armed with the weapons which Athena herself had given him, the hero won the battle, killed Erginus, and compelled the Minyans, the inhabitants of Orchomenus, to pay three times the tribute to the Thebans. As a re-

THE FAMILY TREE OF HERACLES

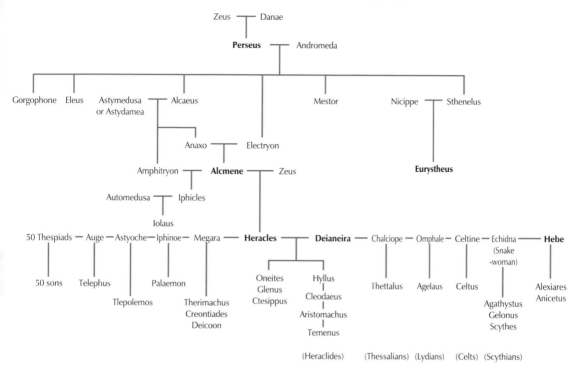

ward, Creon gave him his eldest daughter, Megara, in marriage, and delivered to him the sceptre of the city.

For many years, Heracles lived happily with Megara and their children, ruling Thebes. But the hatred of Hera yet again altered the course of his life. She saw to it that he was possessed by a mania, which drove him out of his mind. In his madness, he believed that his wife and children were his enemies and slew them all with his bow. At this point, Athena intervened: she hit him in the chest with a stone and sent him into a deep death-like sleep.

When he awoke, Heracles had been cured of his madness. Seeing the harm that he had done, he sought the advice of the oracle of Delphi. There he learnt that to expiate his act, he had to serve Eurystheus, who was then the ruler of Mycenae, Tiryns, and Argos, faithfully for twelve years. He was further told that he would carry out unbelievable labours, that he would win immortality, and that he would go to Olympus, together with the other immortals.

The weapons of Heracles

The panoply of Heracles was the work of Hephaestus. On his superb shield, which was clad with silver, gold, and ivory, the god had engraved Phobos and Phonos, Eris and Sphage, herds of goats, and lions, the Battle of the Lapiths and Centaurs, Ares, Athena, and Perseus with the Gorgons. And encircling the shield, he had depicted the boundless Ocean.

The end of Amphitryon and Alcmene

Myth relates that Amphitryon was killed in battle against Erginus. After his death, the gods sent Alcmene to the Isles of the Blest, where she married Rhadamanthus, son of Zeus and brother of Minos.

Labours of Heracles in the Peloponnese -1

Putting aside his club, Heracles attempts to cut off the twelve heads of the Lernaean Hydra (water-snake) with a sickle. Iolaus, on the right, is burning the roots of these heads with torches, so that they will not sprout again. (Red-figure stamnos - psykter, 480 - 470 BC).

Heracles wrestles with the Lion of Nemea at close quarters, since the beast was impervious to weapons. (Black-figure amphora, c. 510 BC).

*I*n accordance with the instructions of the oracle, Heracles had to carry out the orders of Eurystheus for twelve whole years. During that time, the hero completed twelve difficult missions - his 'Labours'. The first task which Eurystheus imposed upon him was to kill the Lion of Nemea. This beast, the offspring of Echidna and the dog Orthus, tore apart, unimpeded, men and animals, since nothing, not even iron, could pierce its hide. So Heracles girded on his weapons and set out for the haunts of the lion. As he was passing through the grove of Nemea, he cut himself a thick branch of wild olive and made himself a heavy club, a weapon which he was rarely to be without in the future. Eventually he reached the lion's cave. Man and beast wrestled for many hours, until Heracles managed to get the lion's neck in a deadly stranglehold and choked the life out of it. In commemoration of his victory, Heracles stipulated that games should be held at Nemea. These were the famous Nemean Games, in which the victors were crowned with wild parsley. Heracles skinned the lion, using its own claws for this purpose, and from then on wore the skin, with the head serving as a helmet and the rest covering his back.

Heracles' second task was to destroy the Lernean Hydra, a monster with nine snake heads, the offspring of Typhon and Echidna, whose poisonous breath burnt up everything before it: plants, animals, and even men. This time, Heracles did not go alone

As Heracles was eating and drinking with his friend the Centaur Pholus, the aroma of the meal reached the other Centaurs, who, maddened by this, attacked Heracles, throwing at him stones and pieces of wood. (Red-figure kylix, c. 500 BC).

Heracles and the Centaurs

On his way to capture the Erymanthine Boar, Heracles met with the Centaur Pholus, who invited him to his cave and provided him with food. However, Pholus opened a jar of wine which belonged to all the Centaurs, and its aroma attracted his companions, who began to gather in an ugly mood. A battle followed in which Heracles slew many of the Centaurs with his poisoned arrows. Pholus, out of curiosity, drew one of the arrows from a wound in the body of one of the dead, but it slipped from his fingers and wounded his leg, causing his death. Heracles, saddened by the loss of the good Centaur, buried him under a mountain in Arcadia, thereafter called Pholoe.

to the lake at Lerna: he took with him his beloved nephew Iolaus, the son of his brother Iphicles. When the monster emerged, the hero, armed with a sharp sickle, began to cut off its heads, one by one. But his labour was in vain: in the place of each head which he cut off another two promptly grew. At this crucial moment, he summoned the aid of Iolaus. Now, as soon as Heracles cut off a head, Iolaus burnt the wound with a blazing torch, so that it would not be replaced. The middle head of the Hydra was immortal, so Heracles buried it in the earth and put a huge rock on top of it. Then he dipped his arrows in the gall of the dead monster, thus making them fatally poisonous.

The third command of Eurystheus to Heracles was that he should take alive the Erymanthine Boar, a fearful wild boar which lived on Mt Erymanthus in Arcadia. The hero doggedly hunted the beast until it was exhausted, and so managed to capture it. He then lifted it on to his shoulders and returned to Mycenae with it. The spectacle so frightened Eurystheus that he hastened to hide in a large bronze storage jar, buried in the earth, which he had specially installed for such emergencies.

In this picture, Heracles, with the boar on his shoulders, has arrived at the palace of Eurystheus, who, terrified, has run to hide in a storage jar. On the right, Athena too seems to be appalled by the beast, while Hermes has appeared, also on the right, to calm everyone down. (Black-figure amphora, c. 510 BC).

Labours of Heracles
in the Peloponnese -2

Heracles attacks the Stymphalian Birds, some of which are flying while others swim in the lake, with a sling. (Black-figure amphora, c. 530 BC).

The next requirement of Eurystheus was that Heracles should bring back alive a hind with golden horns which lived on Mt Cerynea in Achaea and was sacred to the goddess Artemis. This hind not only had golden horns: it had feet as swift as the wind, so that Heracles spent a whole year hunting it, and it was only by wounding it lightly with an arrow that he was able to capture it. On his way back to Mycenae, he met Artemis, who was enraged when she saw that he had taken her sacred animal. But Heracles explained to her that this was on the orders of Eurystheus, and the goddess, mollified, allowed him to continue on his way.

There was, in those days, a city in northern Arcadia called Stymphalus, and near it a lake, Stymphalis. This was the refuge of certain wild birds which had iron wings which they were able to fire like arrows. The extermination of these dangerous creatures was the fifth labour of Heracles. The hero's first problem was to find a way of flushing them out of the dense vegetation of the lake. Here Athena came to his aid by giving him two bronze castanets. With the sound of these, Heracles so startled the birds that they began to emerge from the foliage in their thousands. The hero was then able to aim his arrows, killing most of them. Those which survived flew far away, thus ridding the place of their destructive presence.

Heracles has pinned the Hind of Cerynea down to the ground, and is attempting to cut off its golden horn. (Red-figure kylix, c. 480 BC).

The scene of the sixth labour of Heracles was Elis, whose king was Augeas, son of Helios (the Sun). This king had so many herds of cattle and flocks of sheep that their dung covered the whole country so that the fields could no longer be cultivated. So Eurystheus ordered Heracles to cleanse the country of Augeas in one day, using his own hands. Heracles, therefore, presented himself to the king and told him that he would clear away the dung, without telling him that this was the command of Eurystheus. Augeas, who did not believe that one man could carry out such a task, promised him as a reward a part of his kingdom and a tenth of his flocks. But he did not reckon with the hero's cunning. Heracles, having dug a deep ditch through the middle of the fields and the stables of Augeas, diverted into it the waters of the Alpheus and Peneus, so that in a few hours the rushing stream of the two rivers had swept all the dung into the sea. However, Augeas, who had in the meantime discovered that Heracles was under an obligation to perform this labour, was unwilling to give him the agreed reward. Nor did Eurystheus, when he learnt of the device which Heracles had employed, wish to acknowledge his achievement.

The war with Augeas

When Augeas refused to reward Heracles for his labour, his son Phyleus recognised the injustice of this, and sided with the hero. Augeas, greatly angered by this, drove his son out of the country together with Heracles. But the hero did not remain idle: he collected together an army and, after many adventures, succeeded in defeating the Elians and killing Augeas. He then summoned back Phyleus from the island of Dulichium, where he had taken refuge, and made him ruler over Elia. So that men should remember this victory, Heracles instituted games, to be held at Olympia every four years - the Olympic Games.

Labours of Heracles
at the ends of the earth -1

Relief depiction of the struggle of Heracles with the bull of Cnossus. (Metope from the Temple of Zeus at Olympia, 470 - 456 BC).

W hen Zeus fell in love with Europa, some say that he changed himself into a bull, and carrying the girl on his back, took her as far as Crete. However, another account says that the god and Europa both travelled on the back of a real bull. This bull wandered freely about the island, until the gods afflicted it with madness and it began to cause great damage. So it was to Crete that Heracles was obliged to go this time, to capture the enraged bull. After chasing it from place to place, he was able to seize it by the horns, to tie it up, and to deliver it to Eurystheus, who was deeply impressed by the beauty of the beast and made ready to dedicate it to Hera, as he had promised. But the goddess was unwilling to accept a gift which would result in increasing the fame of Heracles even further. So Eurystheus released the bull, which, after many wanderings, found its way to Marathon. There it continued to wreak destruction, until it fell into the hands of Theseus, the great hero of Athens, who sacrificed it to Delphinios Apollo.

The eighth command of Eurystheus to Heracles was that he should bring to him alive the horses of Diomedes, son of Ares, who was king of a savage and warlike people, the Bistones, in Thrace. These horses breathed fire from their nostrils and were so fierce that they fed on human flesh. When Heracles arrived at the palace of Diomedes, he killed the guards, and hustled away the horses, which he took to the seashore, near his ship, where he left his friend Abderus to guard them. In the meantime, Diomedes disovered what had happened and summoned the Bistones to help him drive out the invaders. On this, Heracles

This small group in bronze shows Heracles to have tamed two of the man-eating horses of Diomedes.

Heracles, now the enemy of the Amazons, has seized the Amazon by her headgear and has immobilised her by treading on her foot. (Metope of Temple E at Selinunte, 470 - 460 BC).

The Amazons

The Amazons were a warlike race, consisting only of women, who ruled, trained, hunted, and fought. Either there were no men at all, or, if there were, their position was that occupied by women among other peoples. If their children were girls, the Amazons cut off their right breast, so that it should not hinder them in battle. If they were boys, they twisted their arms and legs so that they could not be fighters, but instead carried out menial tasks. The country of the Amazons was believed by most people to be in Asia Minor, but views about its location differed.

and his companions turned back to meet them in battle. As soon as the conflict was ended, with Diomedes dead and his men scattered, the hero returned to his ship, where he discovered to his horror that the horses had torn Abderus apart. Deeply mourning, Heracles buried his friend, founding a city called Abdera in his honour. The horses he took in chains to Mycenae.

The next wish of Eurystheus was to acquire the girdle of Hippolyta, queen of the legendary Amazons. When Heracles had gathered together a large force of brave warriors, he set sail for the city of Themiscyra, near the Black Sea, where the Amazons lived. Hippolyta gave a friendly welcome to the hero, and promised to give him her girdle. But Hera, disguised as an Amazon, began to charge him with having come to seize power. The other Amazons, believing this, immediately jumped on their horses and with savage war-cries galloped to the harbour. When Heracles saw these armed women, he thought that Hippolyta had set a trap for him. In the battle which followed, the hero slew many of the Amazons, including Hippolyta, took the girdle, and returned, in triumph once again, to the palace of Eurystheus.

The voluntary giving of the girdle of Hippolyta by the Amazons is the subject of this picture. Here, Heracles, shown as young and sitting on a rock, is looking at the girdle which the Amazon is giving him. (Lucanian hydria, c. 430 BC).

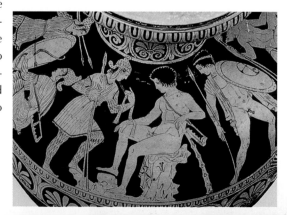

Labours of Heracles
at the ends of the earth -2

In this depiction, Heracles is attacking the three-bodied Geryones with his sword, while the latter's shepherd, Eurytion, wounded by Heracles, is on the point of death on the ground. Athena, on the left, encourages her protegé, while on the right, Iolaus (?) runs away in terror. (Black-figure amphora, c. 540 BC).

Atlas brings Heracles the Apples of the Hesperides, while he holds up the heavens on his shoulders. His protector, Athena, helps him by supporting the firmament with her hand. (Metope of the Temple of Zeus at Olympia, 470 - 456 BC).

*I*n the farthest West, beyond the Ocean, there was an island called Erythia. There lived Geryones, son of Chrysaoras and the Oceanid Callirhoe, a fearful monster with three bodies and three heads. Geryones possessed a herd of fine red cattle which was guarded by a son of Ares, Eurytion, and Orthus, a dog with two heads and a snake for a tail. So Heracles set out, at the behest of Eurystheus, to seize the cattle of Geryones. After having to deal with malefactors and wild animals, he arrived at the channel which divides Europe from Africa, where, to commemorate his journey, he set up two great columns - 'the Pillars of Hercules'. Then, thanks to the Sun, who lent him the golden goblet in which he himself travelled at night, he crossed the Ocean and came to Erythia. Without losing any time, he killed Orthus and Eurytion with his club, and laid low Geryones, who had hastened to protect his herd, with an arrow. Thus the hero was able to return to Mycenae with the cattle of Geryones.

The next task imposed upon Heracles was to bring to the upper world the guard-dog of Hades, Cerberus, a monster with three dog's heads and a tail which ended in the head of a snake. So the hero passed through one of the entrances to the Underworld, a cave on Cape Taenarus. There he found Charon and forced him to take him in his boat to the kingdom of the dead. There he presented himself to Pluto and Persephone and sought their permission to take Cerberus. Pluto agreed to this, on condition that no weapon should be used. As

Heracles presents to Eurystheus the huge Cerberus, with his three dog heads and the snakes rearing up menacingly on his heads and feet. Eurystheus, in his fear, hides in a storage jar. (Caeretan hydria, c. 520 BC).

According to a variant of this myth, Heracles gained possession of the apples by killing the dragon which guarded them - here shown wound round the trunk of the tree - or by persuading the Hesperides to give them to him. The hero is sitting on his lion skin, holding his club in his right hand. (Vase of the 5th century BC).

The Apples of the Hesperides

At the marriage of Zeus with Hera, Mother Earth gave the bride some superb golden apples, symbols of eternal youth and immortality. Hera, delighted with the gift, gave orders that their seed should be planted in the garden of the Hesperides. In this way the trees which grew the golden apples those which Heracles had to take to Eurystheus - were planted.

it turned out, Heracles was able to subdue the beast with his own hands, present it to Eurystheus, and then take it back to Hades, as he had promised Pluto.

The last task of Heracles was to steal the Golden Apples of the Hesperides. This wonderful fruit was in the garden of the gods, in the far West, where the Hesperides, the sweetly-spoken daughters of Night, lived, and was guarded by a huge snake with a hundred heads, by the name of Ladon. On his journey, Heracles passed through many countries, coming eventually to the Caucasus, where he killed the eagle which used to eat the liver of Prometheus, and set the Titan free. In his gratitude, Prometheus advised him to seek the help of his brother Atlas, who supported the heavens on his shoulders, near the garden of the Hesperides. Heracles followed this advice; whereupon Atlas asked him to hold up the heavens for a while, went himself to the garden, and, with help of the Hesperides, who put the snake to sleep with magic herbs, picked three golden apples.

But when he returned, he had formed a plan of leaving Heracles supporting the heavens for ever. The hero pretended to agree to this, but asked Atlas to help him to put a cushion on his shoulders, since he was unaccustomed to the weight. And so Atlas was tricked, since, as soon as he lifted up the heavens, Heracles slipped out from underneath, took the famous apples, and fled. He had now completed his twelfth labour.

Other feats of Heracles

On his way to bring back the Apples of the Hesperides, Heracles passed through Libya, where he heard about the giant Antaeus, the king of that country and the son of Poseidon and Ge, who possessed vast muscular strength. The hero wished to measure his strength against him and challenged him to a duel. In the picture, Heracles has immobilised him with a skilful hold. (Attic red-figure krater, signed by the vase-painter Euphronius, c. 515 BC).

Over and above his great labours, Heracles performed many other brave and good deeds, not because he was forced to do so, but because he always put his strength and courage at the service of mankind. Thus, when he was travelling from country to country in search of the Golden Apples of the Hesperides, he killed Cycnus, son of Ares, who was in the habit of ambushing travellers on their way to Delphi to consult the oracle, robbing them of their votive offerings, and beheading them. He also killed Busiris, King of Egypt, who sacrificed to Zeus all strangers who visited his country.

The hero also fought the giant Antaeus, son of Poseidon and Ge, who ruled over Libya. This bloodthirsty king challenged any strangers who passed that way to a wrestling match and, since he was endowed with superhuman strength, killed them and added their skulls to his collection, with which he was going to build a temple to his father, Poseidon. When Heracles heard of the barabarous practices of Antaeus, he went and sought him out, and challenged him to a duel. For Antaeus, who had thought that this was just another opponent like the rest, the contest proved difficult. But nor could Heracles beat Antaeus as long as the latter had his feet on the ground, from which he drew fresh power. In the end, however, the hero lifted him high in the air, thus cutting off his contact with the earth, and squeezed him so tight that he crushed his bones. In a little while, the giant Antaeus was lying dead on the ground.

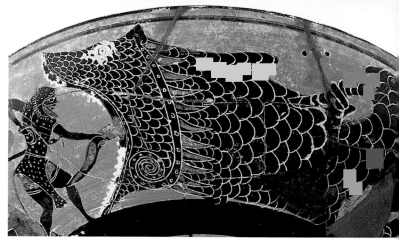

Heracles has approached the great sea-monster which Poseidon has sent to Troy to punish its king, Laomedon, and is attempting to exterminate it by cutting off its tongue with a sickle. (Black-figure kylix, c. 540 BC).

This is a depiction of the quarrel between Apollo and Heracles over the tripod of Delphi, a subject which probably symbolises the conflict between Delphi and the people of Crisa during the First Sacred War. (Red-figure amphora, 530 - 520 BC).

Heracles has seized by the leg one of the Egyptians of King Busiris and is preparing to throw him. The rest, with their racial characteristics satirised, tremble before the supernatural powers of Heracles. (Red-figure pelike, c. 470 BC).

One of the legendary achievements of Heracles was the taking of Troy. The story started when Poseidon, to punish King Laomedon for not having paid him for the building of the city's walls, sent a terrible sea monster, which devoured men and animals. Laomedon then sought an oracle at Delphi; the answer which he received was that to appease the wrath of Poseidon, he would have to choose by lot one of the children of the city as prey for the sea monster. Unfortunately for him, the lot fell upon his daughter Hesione. In his despair, Laomedon announced that he would give his famous immortal horses, a gift from his father, Zeus, to whoever could rescue his daughter and the city. But when Heracles succeeded in killing the sea monster, Laomedon refused to keep his promise. So the hero gathered together an army, took Troy, and killed its king. But he allowed Hesione to redeem one prisoner, and she chose her brother Podarces, who from that point on was called Priam (from *priamai* = buy), the tragic king of the Trojan War, who saw his city rased to the ground by the army of the Achaeans.

The theft of the tripod

At one time, Heracles in a fit of madness committed murder. So he went to the oracle of Apollo at Dephi to ask the Pythia how he could be delivered from this sickness which had seized him again. But the priestess refused to give him an oracle because she regarded him as defiled by murder, and he, in a rage, snatched the oracular tripod, intending to set up his own oracle. Apollo set off in pursuit of him to recover the tripod and caught up with him, and soon god and hero were embroiled in a struggle. In the end, Zeus put an end to the quarrel between his sons by hurling a thunderbolt in between them, and the tripod was returned to its lawful owner.

The end of Heracles

The conflict between Heracles and the Centaur Nessus.
(Attic black-figure amphora, 615 - 605 BC).

*I*n the course of his life, Heracles made many women his own. One of these was Deianeira, whom he married because he had promised her brother Meleager, who he met in Hades, that he would do so. On one of his journeys, the couple wanted to cross the River Euenus with the help of the Centaur Nessus. Heracles let Nessus put Deianeira on his back and go first to the opposite bank. In the middle of the river, however, the Centaur attempted to ravish the woman, and so Heracles shot and killed him with an arrow. When the Centaur realised that he was dying, he told Deianeira to collect his blood because it would serve as a magic love filtre which would keep any rival far from the heart of her husband.

A little later, Heracles learnt that Eurytus, a king who lived at Oechalia, near Eretria, intended to marry his daughter Iole to the winner of an archery contest, and decided to take part. The hero beat Eurytus, but he refused to hand over Iole, on the grounds that Heracles might be seized with another fit of madness, as he had been when he killed Megara and his children. To begin with, Heracles contained his anger and left. But after various escapades, he returned to take his revenge; he conquered Oechalia, slew Eurytus and his sons, and sent Iole under escort to the palace where he lived with

Heracles has risen again from the pyre, high on Oete, where his corruptible body has been burnt and where his trunk still smoulders. Athena is taking him in a chariot to join the immortals, in recognition of the good works he has performed. (Red-figure pelike, c. 450 BC).

The Heraclids

The descendants of Heracles, the Heraclids, were persecuted by Eurystheus and took refuge at Marathon in Attica. Later, they attempted to return to the Peloponnese and re-establish themselves on the land of their fathers, but were unsuccessful. They therefore sought an oracle at Delphi, where they were told that they must wait for the "third fruiting". Initially, the Heraclids interpreted this to mean the third year, but after some unsuccessful attempts to invade the Peloponnese, the oracle revealed to them that it had meant the third generation. And so it came to pass, many years later, when Tissamenus, son of Orestes and grandson of Agamemnon, was king, that the descendants of Heracles flooded into the Peloponnese and conquered all its cities.

Deianeira.

When Deianeira discovered who Iole was, she was wildly jealous. So she sent Heracles, who was in Euboea, a tunic smeared with the blood of Nessus. As soon as Heracles put on the tunic, it stuck to him, causing him appalling pain. Howling with agony, he tried to take it off, but he pulled away with it whole pieces of his own flesh. When, meanwhile, Deianeira was told of the harm she had caused, she committed suicide. Heracles now realised that his end was near, and so he asked his first-born son by Deianeira, Hyllus, to take him to the summit of Oete. There he told his servants to collect together a pile of wood and to put him on it; his son was then to set light to it. But Hyllus could not bring himself to obey. However, Philoctetes arrived at this point and agreed to fulfil his wishes. As a reward, Heracles gave him his bow and arrows, and immediately Philoctetes set fire to the wood. But Heracles was not destined to be burnt. Suddenly it started to thunder and lighten, while at the same time a great cloud shrouded the pyre. When the cloud broke up, those present saw to their amazement that there was no sign of the hero. In this cloud he had ascended to Olympus, where he was reconciled with Hera and married the goddess of youth, Hebe. Thus Heracles became immortal, and soon all the Greeks began to honour him as a god.

The goddess Athena
visits Heracles as he
reclines on a luxurious
couch. (Attic 'bilingual'
amphora, attributed to
the Andocides Painter,
c. 515 BC).

Achilles and Ajax playing draughts. (Attic black-figure amphora, signed by the potter and vase-painter Exekias, c. 530 BC).

Theseus

Theseus drags the dying Minotaur out of the Labyrinth (Interior of a red-figure kylix, 440-430).

A egeus, King of Athens, though twice married, had not been deemed worthy to acquire a successor. He therefore decided to seek the advice of the oracle of Delphi. However, the reply which he received was obscure: "take care not to open your wineskin before you reach Athens". Leaving Delphi, Aegeus visited Troezen, where his friend Pittheus was king, to ask his opinion about the oracle. Pittheus, it would seem, understood its meaning. He got Aegeus drunk and then arranged for him to sleep with his daughter Aethra, who the same night had also slept with Poseidon.

When Aegeus learnt that Aethra was expecting a child, he was delighted, but, in spite of this, had to hasten back to Athens, because he was afraid of his brother Pallas and his fifty sons, who coveted the throne and were engaged in attempts to overthrow him. But before he went, he hid his sandals and his sword under a rock. He then told Aethra that if her child was a boy, she was not to tell him of his origins before he reached adolescence. Only then was she to show him the rock and, by lifting it, reveal to him who his father was, advising him to go to find him at Athens.

Aethra did have a son, and called him Theseus. Theseus, son of Aegeus, or, possibly, of Poseidon, grew up at Troezen, with Aethra and Pittheus. It became clear

Theseus greets his mortal father, Aegeus, while his mother, Aethra, touches him with tenderness. Behind Theseus, his divine father, Poseidon, watches the scene. (Red-figure amphora, c. 470 - 460 BC).

The origins of Theseus

Theseus was descended from Erichthonius, the Athenian king who was born from the seed of Hephaestus which was spilled on the earth when he attempted to rape Athena. Erichthonius was succeeded by his son Pandion. Next, the son of Pandion, Erechtheus, became king. He married Praxithea, granddaughter of Cephisus, and had seven children by her. One of the daughters of Erechtheus, Oreithyia, was abducted by Boreas, a personification of the strong wind, and married to him. Another, Chthonia, died for her country when Erechtheus was told by an oracle that for the city to be spared the impending attack of the Eleusinians, he must sacrifice one of his daughters. Aegeus, father of Theseus, was the grandson of one of the sons of Erechtheus, Cecrops.

from an early age that the child would be courageous. Once, when Heracles was visiting the palace of Pittheus, before sitting down to eat, he took off his lion's skin and laid it on the ground. All the children of Troezen ran away in terror. Theseus alone, who was just seven years old, thinking that it was a real lion, snatched up an axe and rushed to kill it.

As soon as he reached the right age, and since he seemed to be intelligent and strong, Aethra took him to the place where the gifts of Aegeus were hiddened. Theseus lifted the rock with ease and listened to his mother's account of his origins. He then took his father's sandals and sword and set out for Athens. In vain Aethra and Pittheus attempted to persuade him to travel by sea. He, impatient to gain glory for his feats, like the great hero Heracles, chose to travel by the land route, which was full of danger.

Aegeus, father of Theseus and King of Athens, in despair because he had no male heir, went to seek the advice of the oracle at Delphi. In the picture, he is listening carefully to Themis, an old deity of the oracle. (Interior of a red-figure kylix, 440 - 430 BC).

Theseus
on the way to Athens

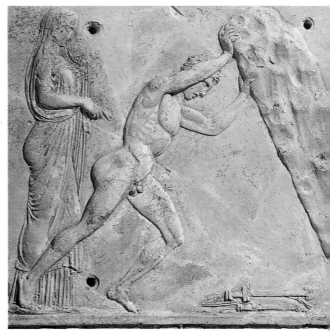

Theseus, guided by his mother, Aethra, lifted the rock with ease, found his father's gifts - the sword and the sandals left there by Aegeus as a means of recognition - and set out to Athens to find his father. (Roman earthernware relief, 1st century AD).

On the road to Athens, Theseus met with a number of malefactors. At Epidaurus, he came across Periphetes, son of Hephaestus, who killed passers-by with an iron club. Theseus wrestled with him, killed him, and kept the club for himself. Cenchreae, near the Isthmus, was the home of Sinis, son of Poseidon, also called Pityocamptes ('Pine-bender') because of the fearful way he had devised of killing travellers. His practice was to bend together the tops of two pine trees and tie any stranger he came across between them. He would then let the trees go, so that as they sprang back into their upright position, they would pull his victim apart. But his meeting with Theseus was to prove fatal. The hero tied him to the bent pine trees, and so this criminal met with the end he deserved.

Theseus then went on to Crommyon, where the town of Aghii Theodori stands today, where he killed the wild sow Phaea, daughter of Typhon and Echidna, which had been causing widespread damage in that area.

His next stop was at the Scironian Rocks - today called Kakia Skala. There Sciron, son of Corinthus and grandson of Pelops, forced passers-by to bend down and wash his feet. As soon as they did so, Sciron would give them a great kick and send them over the cliff into the sea, where they would be devoured by an enormous turtle. Theseus punished him by sending him to the same fate over the cliff.

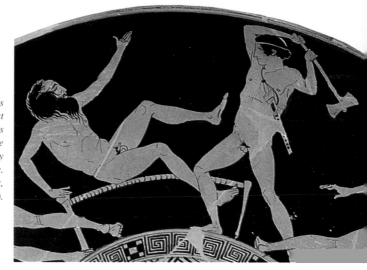

In this picture, Theseus is threatening Procrustes, the last criminal whom he met on his way to Athens - he lived on the Sacred Way, near present-day Dafni - with an axe. (Interior of a red-figure kylix, c. 440 - 430 BC).

At Eleusis, Theseus performed yet another feat. He attacked Cercyon, son of Poseidon, who challenged travellers to a wrestling match to the death. Lifting him high in the air, he dashed him to the ground and killed him.

Theseus's last encounter was with Procrustes, who lived on the Sacred Way, near the present-day Dafni.

On the road to Athens, Theseus encountered various malefactors. At Cenchreae, near the Isthmus, he killed Sinis the Pine-bender, by bending down the top of two pines and tying him to them - in the same way, that is, that Sinis himself killed travellers. (Interior of an Attic red-figure kylix, c. 490 BC).

Procrustes, also a son of Poseidon, was in the habit of inviting in those who passed by, ostensibly to offer them hospitality. But he had two beds made up, one long and one short. Those who were short in stature he forced to lie down on the long bed and beat them with a hammer so as to stretch them. Tall strangers were put on the short bed, where he cut off those limbs which were too long for it. But he was not able to subject Theseus to this treatment. On the contrary, he met with his own death at the hands of the hero, on the murderous bed which he had devised.

After all these adventures, Theseus at last passed through the gates of Athens and headed for the palace of his father.

The Bull of Marathon

The wild bull which Heracles had brought from Crete had finally settled at Marathon in Attica, where it was causing havoc. When Theseus had established himself in Athens, he resolved to rid the country of this appalling beast. But as he was on his way to Marathon, it suddenly came on to rain heavily and he sheltered in the house of an old woman called Hecale. The next day, he continued on his way, and managed to capture the bull alive. On his return, he visited the home of Hecale, but the hospitable old woman had in the meantime died. After parading the bull in triumph around Athens, Theseus sacrificed it to Delphinios Apollo. He then instituted honours in memory of Hecale and gave her name to a village in Attica.

87

Theseus
in the palace of Aegeus

Here Aegeus is shown giving, on the instructions of Medea, who stands behind him dispassionately, the cup containing poison to Theseus, without it having occurred to him that this could be his son. (Earthernware relief, 1st / 2nd century AD).

When Theseus reached the palace of his father, Aegeus, who had already heard of his achievements, the latter entertained him without suspecting that he was his son. But his wife, Medea, who was a witch, realised this and wanted to get rid of him, since she feared that he would take the throne from her own son by Aegeus, Medus. She therefore persuaded the king to invite Theseus to a meal and to poison him. Up to that moment, Theseus had not revealed his true identity, but at table he produced his father's sword, as if to cut the meat. As soon as Aegeus saw it, he threw away the cup containing the poison which he had been going to give him, and, by dint of various questions, established that he was indeed his son. Aegeus at once called together all the citizens and presented Theseus to them. They accepted him joyfully, since they had already learnt about his heroism. After the recognition of Theseus by Aegeus, Medea was compelled to take Medus and to flee to Asia Minor.

The arrival of Theseus in Athens greatly disturbed Pallas and his fifty sons, who had believed that their uncle was without an heir and that they would succeed him on the throne. So they now decided to take power by force. They divided themselves into two groups, one of which went quite openly to the centre of Athens, while the rest hid and set up an ambush. Theseus, however, was informed of their movements

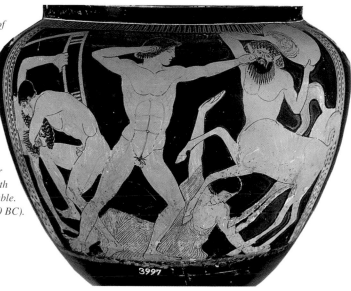

At the marriage of Pirithous, King of the Lapiths, the Centaurs who were guests got drunk and made advances to the Lapith women. In this picture, Theseus, the friend and valued supporter of Pirithous, punches a Centaur who is attacking him with a pot, treading on a Lapith woman who has fallen to the ground. On the left, a Lapith, perhaps Pirithous, attempts to overcome another Centaur who has attacked him with the use of a table. (Red-figure krater, 475 - 450 BC).

The Battle of the Lapiths and the Centaurs

When he married Hippodamia, Pirithous invited the Centaurs, who were his half-brothers, since they had the same father, King Ixion, but a different mother, to the wedding. At the celebrations, the Centaurs consumed large quantities of wine and got drunk. One of them, Eurytion, in his drunkenness attempted to ravish the bride, while the rest of the Centaurs followed his example and attacked the wives of the Lapiths. A major conflict followed, in which Theseus, who was also a guest at the wedding, also took part. The Lapiths emerged victorious, having killed many of the Centaurs and driven the rest far from the places where they lived.

and so was able to surprise and kill those who had hidden. The rest managed to make their escape. At the trial for the murder of the sons of Pallas which followed, the hero was acquitted on the grounds that he had right on his side. It is said that this was the first time that anyone had been tried for the murder of relatives and found innocent.

A little later, Perithous, the great hero of the Lapiths of Thessaly, heard the stories about the heroism of Theseus and decided to put him to the test. For this purpose, he went to Marathon and stole the hero's cattle which were grazing there. Theseus learnt of this and at once set out to find and kill Perithous. But as soon as the two men came face to face, they stopped

Aegeus, King of Athens, welcomes his son Theseus to his homeland. A girl, on the right, holding a wreath, comes to honour the brave hero. (Red-figure skyphos, 475 - 470 BC).

dead in their tracks, each filled with wonder at the good looks and courage of the other. Pirithous was first to give his hand to Theseus and offered to compensate him for the theft of the cattle. The latter proposed that they should become friends and allies. And so Theseus and Pirithous shook hands, setting the seal on a friendship which was to become legendary.

Theseus
and the Minotaur

The most popular of Theseus' labours is shown here: the hero is dragging the dying Minotaur out of the Labyrinth, shown by means of the monumental entrance and the key-pattern decoration, which symbolises its complex maze. On the left, Athena supports the hero. (Interior of an Attic red-figure kylix, c. 420 BC).

Androgeus, son of Minos, King of Crete, once attempted, on the prompting of Aegeus, to deal with the bull of Marathon - the one which was subsequently killed by Theseus - but was the loser in the contest. Thus, Minos, who regarded the Athenians as responsible for the death of his son, declared war on them, conquered them, and required them to send each year - or every nine years - seven youths and seven maidens as fodder for the Minotaur. This monster, with the body of a man and the head of a bull, was the result of the mating of Pasiphae, wife of Minos, with a bull. In his shame, Minos imprisoned the Minotaur in the Labyrinth, the work of Deadalus, a strange maze-like construction from which it was impossible to find one's way out.

When the time came for Athens to pay once again the human tribute to Crete, Theseus volunteered to be one of the seven young men to be thrown to the Minotaur. Aegeus, with many reservations, was forced to give in to his son's wishes, but he gave orders to the captain of the ship which was taking the young people to Crete to replace the black sails with white if they escaped alive. This was to be a sign that Theseus was returning alive and triumphant. As soon as the ship dropped anchor at the island, the goddess Aphrodite performed a miracle: Ariadne, the daughter of King Minos, fell in love with the hero and made up her mind to help him - on condition that Theseus would take her away with him and marry her. Theseus made this promise, and so Ariadne gave

Theseus kills the Minotaur with his sword, thus putting an end to the obligation which the Athenians had had for many years of sending seven boys and seven girls, food for the monster, as tribute to Minos, King of Crete. Four of these young people watch Theseus as he carries out the feat. (Black-figure psykter - amphora, 560 - 540 BC).

On the instructions of Athena, Theseus abandons his beloved Ariadne, yielding to the will of the god Dionysus, who had been enchanted by Ariadne's beauty. In the picture, Theseus stoops to take his sandals from near the sleeping Ariadne in order to follow Hermes, who is showing him the way. (Red-figure kylix, 490 - 480 BC).

him a ball of thread, telling him to fasten one end at the entrance to the Labyrinth and to unwind it as he made his way along its passageways. In this way, he would easily be able to retrace his steps to the entrance. The plan worked: the hero entered the Labyrinth, killed the Minotaur, and, following the thread, found his way out again. Immediately, he made holes in the ship of the Cretans so that they would not be able to pursue him, and left by night together with the children of Athens and Ariadne.

On his way back to Athens, Theseus stopped off for a while on Naxos, where Dionysus, enchanted by the beauty of Ariadne, asked the hero to leave her there for him to marry. But another version of the story says that Theseus, either because he loved another, or because such

Daedalus

Deadalus, the grandson of Erechtheus, was a marvellous architect, sculptor, carftsman, and inventor. He was particularly renowned for his statues, which were so lifelike that people expected them to move. One day, jealous of his nephew Talus, who was equally able, he killed him, and was forced to flee from Athens to Crete. When, however, he constructed the wooden cow which contained Pasiphae so that the bull would mate with her, he aroused the displeasure of Minos, whereupon he made some large wings, like those of a bird, and, taking his son Icarus, whose mother was one of the king's slave girls, they flew away from the island. Icarus, however, flew too close to the sun and the wax with which his father had stuck the wings together melted, with the result that the boy fell and was drowned in what is now called the Icarian Sea.

was the command of Athena, set sail leaving the girl asleep on some beach on the island, where Dionysus saw her and took her to himself. In any case, the ship continued its voyage without Ariadne. But the only problem was that nobody remembered to change the sails. In the meantime, Aegeus went up every day to the Acropolis to look out for the return of his son, and as soon as he saw the ship in the distance with the black sails, he thought Theseus was dead, and, overcome with despair, committed suicide by plunging into the sea. From that time on, the sea in which Aegeus drowned has been called the Aegean.

Theseus as king

Theseus is shown here as the revered ruler who united the demes of Attica and is 'promoted' as an Athenian hero who was a model of rectitude and virtue. (Fragment of a black-figure amphora, 540 - 530 BC).

On the death of Aegeus, Theseus succeeded to the throne of Athens. Up till then, Attica had consisted of many small townships, each with its own centre of administration and rulers. Theseus decided to abolish the local authorities and to establish the city of Athens as a common political centre for the whole of Attica. Similarly, the Athenaea, the festival in honour of the goddess Athena, was renamed the Panathenaea, a name which symbolised this political unification. Theseus was a model king. He refused to govern autocratically, concerned himself with his people, and was noted for his philanthropy.

When he was still a young man, Theseus accompanied Heracles on his campaign to obtain the girdle of Hippolyta. There he fell in love with the Amazon Antiope, took her back with him to Greece, and had a son by her - Hippolytus. But the Amazons, to avenge the abduction of Antiope, came to Athens in an aggressive mood. In the battle which followed, the Amazons were defeated, but Antiope lost her life fighting on the side of Theseus.

After losing his Amazon wife, Theseus married Phaedra, one of the daughters of Minos. When, however, she saw Theseus's beautiful and athletic son, Hippolytus, she fell madly in love with him. Having tried in vain to stifle her wayward feelings for him, she wrote him a letter confessing her passion. The youth was outraged and re-

In this vase-painting, Heracles attempts to lift Theseus off the throne on which Hades has imprisoned him, together with Pirithous, because they had dared to steal Persephone from him. (Red-figure lekythos, 475 - 450 BC).

Theseus and the Athenians

The heroism of Theseus and his love of Athens and of liberty was such a deeply-rooted article of faith in the souls of the Athenians that in 490 BC, when they were fighting against the Persians at Marathon, they saw the ghost of Theseus fighting at their side.

---

fused to reciprocate her feelings, whereupon Phaedra, fearing that her stepson might reveal the matter to Theseus, killed herself. First, however, she left a letter for Theseus, accusing Hippolytus of having made immoral advances to her. As soon as Theseus read the letter, he cursed his son and drove him out of Athens. At once, Poseidon, who had promised the hero that he would fulfil three wishes for him, sent a wild bull which startled the horses which drew the chariot of Hippolytus. The terrified animals smashed the chariot, while the unfortunate Hippolytus became entangled in the reins and was dragged over the rocks and killed.

At the time of Phaedra's suicide, Theseus had reached the age of fifty. In spite of this, he agreed with Pirithous, who had also lost his wife, that they should both marry daughters of gods. So they went to Sparta, where they met with Helen, the beautiful twelve year old daughter of Zeus and Leda, and abducted her. Later, after they had drawn lots and Theseus had won Helen, they descended to the Underworld to bring back Persephone for Pirithous. But there Pluto tricked them, getting them to sit on the throne of Lethe, from which it was impossible to rise. When Heracles went down to Hades, Theseus had the good fortune to be released by him, but Heracles was unable to do the same for Pirithous.

After this last adventure, Theseus entrusted the rule to Menestheus, a descendant of Erechtheus, and left for Skyros. The king there was Lycomedes, whom Theseus regarded as a friend, but Lycomedes pushed him off a cliff and killed him. And so the life of one of the greatest of the Greek heroes came to an inglorious end.

Jason

The hero Jason supported by the goddess Hera. Detail from a sarcophagus of the Antonine period

*T*yro, daughter of King Salmoneus, after the death of her father, lived in the palace of her uncle, Cretheus, at Iolcus. As she grew up, she fell in love with the river-god Enipeus, but he did not reciprocate her feelings. So every day she was going to his banks and wept. On one of her visits to the river, Poseidon, who was in love with her, took on the appearance of Enipeus, and made her his own. He then revealed himself to her, prophesied that she would give birth to two boys, and ordered her to keep their relationship a secret.

When the time came for her to give birth, Tyro left the palace on the pretext that she was going to the river to wash clothes. There, far from anyone, she brought into the world twin boys, whom she put in the washing-trough, and left to their fate. But the boys, as sons of a god, were not destined to perish and were rescued by a herder of horses, who named them Pelias and Neleus. Later, they were recognised by their mother when she chanced to hear from the herder that he had found them in a washing-trough. In the meantime, Tyro, who had married Cretheus, had produced three other sons: Aeson, Amythaon, and Pheres.

When Cretheus died, Aeson, his lawful heir, should have succeeded to the throne, but Pelias managed to take power by force. Aeson, fearing for the safety of his only son, Jason, pretended that the boy had died and, secretly, in the night, hid him away in the

Pelias, with his two daughters, as he arrives on the steps of the temple to sacrifice to Poseidon the bull which is being led by the young man on the left, suddenly sees the proud stranger who is wearing only one sandal. At the table of sacrifice, next to Jason, stands Pelias's third daughter. (Wall-painting, Pompeii, c. 10 AD).

cave of the wise Centaur Chiron, on Mt Pelion. There, Jason trained his body and mind, and, as soon as he reached the age of twenty, set out to Iolcus to lay claim to power and his father's fortune.

On the way, the young man met with Hera, who appeared in the guise of a frail old woman, who, to test him, asked him to help her to cross the River Anaurus. He showed himself willing, and, lifting her on to his shoulders, carried her over to the other bank. However, in crossing the swollen river, Jason lost one of his sandals. Thus he entered Iolcus with only one sandal.

The citizens of Iolcus, who had gathered to offer sacrifice to Poseidon, were speechless with admiration when they saw this handsome youth with his long blond hair, which made him look like Apollo. By contrast, Pelias, who arrived at that very moment in his chariot, froze in terror as he remembered an old oracle which told him to beware of a man with one sandal. So when Jason asked him to hand over the kingdom to him, he pretended to agree to this, but he made it a condition that Jason should fetch the Golden Fleece from distant Colchis, hoping that he would be lost on this dangerous journey. So Jason, with all the vigour of youth, accepted the cunning king's proposal and began to make ready.

Salmoneus

Aeolus, son of Hellen, who ruled in Aeolis, as Thessaly was once called, had five sons: Cretheus, Athamas, Sisyphus, Salmoneus, and Perieres. One of these, Salmoneus, at one point migrated to Elis together with many of the inhabitants of Aeolis, built a city, called in Salmone, and became its king. However, intoxicated by his power, he began to imagine that he was Zeus himself. In order to punish him, the king of the gods hurled his terrible thunderbolts against him and his people, wiping them out completely. The only one to escape from this fate was the daughter of King Salmoneus, Tyro, whom Zeus himself took to Iolcus in Thessaly, where Cretheus, her father's brother, was king.

95

The Golden Fleece

Phrixus, grasping the right horn of the miraculous ram, flies over the sea. (Red-figure pelike, c. 460 - 450 BC).

Athamas, son of Aeolus and King of Orchomenus in Boeotia, had married a goddess, Nephele, by whom he had two children, Phrixus and Helle. Later, Athamas drove out Nephele and took Ino, one of the daughters of Cadmus, as his wife. She bore him two sons, Learchus and Melicertes. But Ino could not stand the children of Nephele, and so she laid a devious plan to get rid of them. She persuaded the women of the country to roast the seed which the men kept for sowing, without the latter's knowledge. Naturally enough, the next year not even a single ear of corn sprouted on the plains, whereupon Athamas sent emissaries to Delphi to ask the god what he must do to rescue the people from famine. This was the opportunity which Ino had been waiting for. She bribed the emissaries to tell the king that the only way for this evil to be stopped was for Phrixus to be sacrificed on the altar of Zeus. Under pressure from the despairing farmers, Athamas was forced to lead his son to the slaughter. But at the last moment Nephele sent a golden-fleeced ram which she had been given by Hermes. At once, Phrixus climbed on to its back, together with his sister Helle, and it sped off with them.

Phrixus and Helle travelled thus over sea and land, but, as they were crossing the straits which separate Sigeum from the Thracian Chersonese, Helle slipped off the ram, fell, and was drowned in the waters of the straits, which took her name and came to be called the Hellespont. Phrixus, however, continued his journey, until he came to the eastern shore of the Euxine Sea, to Colchis, where Aeetes, son of

Ino, wife of Athamas, raises an axe against Phrixus, who has already seized by the horn the golden-fleeced ram which is to bear him to distant Colchis. (Red-figure amphora, c. 430 BC).

Phrixus leads the ram to the altar, to sacrifice it to Phyxios Zeus. King Aeetes goes before him. (Lucanian nestoris, c. 330 BC).

Helios (the Sun) and the Oceanid Perseis, and brother of the witch Circe and of Pasiphae, the wife of Minos, was king. Aeetes gave a friendly welcome to the stranger and married him to one of his daughters from his union with the Oceanid Idyia, Chalciope. Phrixus sacrificed the ram to Phyxios Zeus and gave its golden fleece to Aeetes, who hung it in an oak tree, in the grove which was dedicated to the god Ares, and set a snake, as long as a fifty-oared ship, which kept vigil day and night, to guard it.

Leucothea and Palaemon

In order to take revenge on Ino and Athamas, who had agreed to bring up Dionysus, the bastard son of Zeus, Hera drove them out of their minds. And so Athamas unintentionally killed one of his sons, Learchus, taking him for a deer, while Ino, with the other son, Melicertes, was thrown into the sea. But Poseidon and the Nereids took pity on the woman and the child, and not only did they not allow them to drown, but made them deities of the sea. From then on, Ino, who was given the name of Leucothea, and Melicertes, who became Palaemon, represented well-disposed sea spirits who gave their aid to seamen and often rescued them from mortal danger.

The Expedition of the Argonauts

Three of the Argonauts, on board or around the Argo, watch their companions, who are then shown in the continuation of the scene - not included here - engaged in one of their many feats. (Red-figure krater, 400 - 390 BC).

Jason's first concern was to order from the architect Argus a ship with fifty oars. With the help of the goddess Athena, the ship which was produced was strong, but it was also so light that the crew could carry it on their shoulders. It was also remarkably fast, and so it was given the name Argo (= swift). In addition, Athena placed on the prow a piece of wood from the sacred oak at Dodona which could speak with a human voice and make prophecies.

Jason then called together the most renowned heroes of Greece to accompany him in his bold undertaking, which is known as the Expedition of the Argonauts. As soon as the seer Mopsus assured them that the omens were favourable, the Argonauts set out for Colchis. Their first stop was at Lemnos, which they found bereft of men. This situation had come about because Aphrodite, angry with the women of Lemnos because they did not pay her due honour, laid a curse on them that they should smell appallingly, with the result that the men preferred to sleep with the women slaves. The women, neglected in this manner, slaughtered all the male inhabitants of the island and made Hypsipyle, daughter of King Thoas, their ruler. However, through the good offices of Hephaestus, Aphrodite made the Lemnian women desire the Argonauts and sleep with them, so as to ensure the existence of another generation.

After various other adventures, the Argonauts anchored on the southern shore of the Propontis, where they were entertained by Cyzicus, King of the Doliones. But when they were ready to leave, they were caught in a great tempest and forced to turn back. As it was night, the Doliones mistook them for enemies and attacked them. It was only when the fierce battle was over, and Jason had killed Cyzicus, that the two sides realised their terrible mistake, whereupon they mourned the fallen and honoured them with magnifi-

On the right, Argus works with the hammer and chisel, while on the left Athena, Jason's protectress, assists Tiphys (?), the helmsman, to fix the sail on the mast of the miraculous ship Argo. (Roman earthernware relief plaque, first half of the 1st century AD).

In the centre of the scene, the blind seer Phineus, in an Asiatic theatre costume and with a sceptre in his hand, sits in front of a table with the remains of the food which the Harpies have left him. On a lower level, Hermes turns to watch the Harpies depart, while, above him, one of the sons of the north wind, holding a sword, prepares to pursue them. (Lucanian krater, late 5th century BC).

One of the two winged sons of the north wind threatens the terrible Harpies, who are flying above him with the food of Phineus and his wine vessel, with his spear. (Lucanian krater, late 5th century BC).

cent funeral games.

The next stop of the Argo was on the coast of Mysia. There a nymph stole away Hylas, and Heracles, hearing his cries, went off to find him. In the meantime, the Argonauts had embarked and put to sea without noticing that their companions were missing. When they realised this, it was too late to turn back. The voyage continued until the heroes came to the land of the blind seer Phineus, who had been punished by Zeus for giving oracles which were too easily intelligible. Every time he was ready to eat, the Harpies Aello and Ocypete, destructive goddesses of the wind, would swoop down and snatch away his food, seeing to it that the very little which they left him to survive gave off a horrible smell. By a stroke of good fortune, the sons of Boreas, the north wind, drove off these winged monsters, and Phineus, as an act of gratitude, explained to the Argonauts how they could protect themselves against the Symplegades, two facing rocks which came together and parted constantly, crushing any ship which passed between them. His advice was that they should first let a dove fly between the rocks. If the bird escaped unscathed, so would they. This proved true: just as the bird passed through unharmed - except for the loss of a few tail-feathers - so the Argo too passed through with minimal damage and headed for the land of Aeetes.

The catalogue of the Argonauts

Among those who took part in the Expedition of the Argonauts were Peleus, father of Achilles, Telamon, father of Ajax, Laertes and Autolycus, father and grandfather respectively of Odysseus, Meleager and those who had been his companions in the hunting of Calydonian Boar, Orpheus, the renowned singer, Admetus, son of Pheres, Castor and Pollux, brothers of Helen and Clytemnestra, Calais and Zetes, the winged sons of the north wind and Oreithyia, Heracles and his companion Hylas, and the seers Mopsus and Idmon.

Jason at Colchis

Jason, with sword raised, steals the Golden Fleece, while the snake, curled round the tree, unsuspectingly drinks the magic potion given to it by Medea. (Paestum -very probably- krater, early 4th century BC).

As soon as the Argo had dropped anchor at Colchis, Jason presented himself to Aeetes and told him of his origins and the purpose of his voyage. The king, who had been given an oracle to the effect that he would remain in power only as long as the Golden Fleece was hanging on the oak tree in the grove of Ares, decided to put him to death. He therefore told him that he would have what he was looking for if he succeeded in yoking two bulls with bronze hooves, and flames coming from their mouths, ploughing a field with them, sowing the teeth of a dragon, and killing the fully-armed giants who would spring up from the earth.

Jason succeeded in these difficult tasks with the help of the witch Medea, the second daughter of Aeetes, who fell in love with him through the intervention of Hera. The girl brought him first of all a magic unguent which had the power of protecting him from the animals fiery breath. Thus the hero found no difficulty in yoking the bronze-hooved royal bulls, ploughing the field, and sowing the teeth. Then, when he found himself encircled by the giants, he threw a stone among them, as he had been advised to do by the witch. They immediately began to fight among themselves, until they had all killed one another.

Aeetes, who had now begun to fear for his throne, on seeing the hero's feats, wished

Aeetes, seated on a rock with Apsyrtus (?), watches Jason struggling to subdue the bull. (Sarcophagus of the Antonine period).

The episode depicted here is not preserved in any literary tradition. Jason emerges, half-dead, from the mouth of the terrible dragon of Colchis. Athena, fully armed, looks on sympathetically. It seems that the hero, following the advice of the goddess, has entered the belly of the beast to attack it from within, because on the outside it is protected by its invulnerable skin. (Red-figure kylix, 480 - 470 BC).

The musician Orpheus, one of the leading Argonauts, who saved his companions on many occasions by his wise counsels and his exquisite song, goes on to the podium to play his seven-stringed cithara. (Black-figure oinochoe, c. 530 BC).

to subject him to yet another trial. But Medea secretly took the Argonauts to the grove of Ares, put to sleep the guardian dragon by dripping a magic filtre into his eyes, and thus enabled Jason to take the Golden Fleece. All of them, the Argonauts and Medea, embarked upon the Argo and headed for the north-western shores of the Euxine. There they decided to follow the River Ister in order to reach the Adriatic. It is said that Aeetes sent Apsyrtus, his son by his second wife, Eurylyte, to capture them, but he fell into a trap set by Jason and met a tragic end. Another version says that Medea took with her her half-brother, who was still a child. When she realised that her father was pursuing them, she killed Apsyrtus, dismembered him, and threw him into the sea. Naturally, Aeetes stopped the chase to gather together the remains of his much-lamented only son and to give them burial.

Orpheus

According to one variant of the myth, the dragon was put to sleep, by his music, by the Thracian Orpheus, the son of Oeager, the spirit of a river in Thrace, and of the Muse Calliope. It was said that when Orpheus sang, the whole of nature gathered round him: wild animals, fish, even inanimate objects such as stones and trees. On the Argonaut's expedition he was able to help his companions on many occasions, thanks to the power of his music. Once, Orpheus descended into Hades to bring back to life his young wife Eurydice, who had died of a snake bite. Pluto and Persephone, moved by his melodies, allowed Eurydice to follow him, on condition that he should not turn his head to look at her until they had arrived back on earth. Orpheus, however, was not able to contain himself, and so the girl had to remain for ever in the world of shades.

The return of the Argo

The witch Medea, wearing a gorgeous Oriental costume and holding the box with her magic potions. (Detail - red-figure krater, 400 - 390 BC).

*H*aving escaped from the Cholcians, the Argonauts came to the Adriatic and set sail south. They were nearing Corcyra (Corfu), when a strong wind, sent by Hera, drove them back north again. At this point, the Argo, which had the power of human speech, advised them to take refuge with Circe, sister of Aeetes, who lived on the island of Aeaea, somewhere on the west coast of what is today Italy, so that she could purify them from the murder of Apsyrtus, which had angered Zeus. Obedient to the will of the god, the Argonauts sailed up the River Eridanus, came to Rhodanus, and from there entered the Tyrrhenian Sea. Before long, the Argo anchored at the island of Circe, who performed the necessary ceremonies, and then the heroes continued on their way, purified.

Then, after they had escaped from the island of the Sirens, they had to pass the Wandering Rocks, which, wrapped in flames and smoke, voyaged over the sea, following the direction of the wind. The foam of the waves which covered them led seamen astray, so that their vessels were smashed against them. With the help of Thetis and the other Nereids, the Argo managed to pass by the Wandering Rocks and to reach the island of the Phaeacians - Corcyra. But some Colchians soon arrived there and asked the king of the island, Alcinous, to hand Medea over to them. But thanks to the intervention of Queen Arete, Jason and Medea were married, and the Colchians dropped their claim.

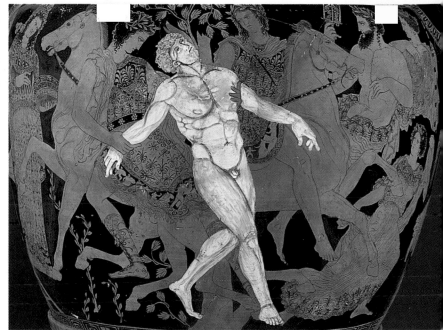

As the blood has almost drained from his vein, the bronze giant Talus falls, dying, into the hands of the Dioscuri, Castor and Pollux. The tragic end of the unsleeping custodian of Crete is watched by Poseidon and Amphitrite, on the right, and Medea, on the left. (Red-figure krater, 400 - 390 BC).

After leaving Corcyra behind them, the heroes were driven by high seas to the shores of north Africa. In despair because their vessel was grounded in the sand, they went on to the dry land. There the gods informed them that if they were to see their homeland again, they would have to carry the Argo on their shoulders across the Libyan Desert. After walking for twelve days and nights and a number of escapades, they reached Lake Tritonis, and from there were once again able to take to the open sea. The next stop of the Argo was Crete, where Jason and his companions had to face Talus, the gift of Hephaestus to Minos. Talus was a bronze giant who made the round of the island three times a day and prevented ships from approaching the shore. The life of Talus depended upon a vein, full of blood, which terminated in his ankle and was closed with a bronze nail. Medea told him, therefore, that if he took out the nail, he would become immortal. Talus believed her and, as soon as his blood had all escaped, fell down dead.

When the Argonauts had left Crete, they were suddenly plunged into a thick darkness, accompanied by terrible weather. They prayed to Apollo, and the god, raising high his golden bow, shed light on the sea. At once they saw a small island nearby, to which they gave the name of Anaphe (from a verb meaning to come to light). There they spent the night, before once again spreading their sails and, without any more major difficulties, reaching Iolcus.

The Sirens

The Sirens, who lived on the island of Anthemoessa in the Tyrrhenian Sea, were beings with a human head and the body of a bird. Their father was said to have been the sea god Phorcys or the River Achelous, while their mother was either Chthon (the earth) or the Muse Terpsichore. The Sirens sang so sweetly that sailors used to leave their ships to go to listen to them. Beguiled, they forgot to eat and drink, and so eventually died. When the Argo drew close to Anthemoessa, Orpheus began to play his lyre and sing. His melodies so entranced the Argonauts that they paid no attention to the Sirens and continued their voyage unharmed.

Jason and Medea

In the centre of the scene, Alcestis, the only one of the daughters of Pelias who has not believed the deceitful words of Medea, looks in horror at the knife held by one of her sisters and raises her hand to her mouth in dismay. Another daughter runs towards the right, her hands stretched out in horror. (Red-figure hydria, c. 465 BC).

*I*t was still night when Jason and his companions dropped anchor in a bay near Iolcus. They were told immediately that Pelias had not only no intention of keeping his promise, but had already killed Aeson and all Jason's relatives. As soon as he heard this, Jason swore to take revenge for their untimely death. The punishment of Pelias was undertaken by Medea, who was an expert in poisons and magic herbs. She covered her skin with an ointment to make her appear wrinkled, dyed her hair white and, dressed like one of the priestesses of Artemis, entered the palace. There she presented herself to the king, and revealed to him that Artemis has greatly pleased with his piety and wished to reward him by giving him back his youth. Then she told his daughters that in order for their father to become youthful once again, they must kill him in his sleep, dismember him and boil him in a pot with magic potions which she would give them. In order to convince them, she did exactly the same with an old ram, but, while the animal was chopped up in the cauldron, she made them see the image of a lamb. Thus the girls were deluded and robbed their father of his life with their own hands. After all this, Jason abdicated from the throne of Iolcus, handing over power to Pelias's only son, Acastus. He himself took Medea and their two children and went to live at Corinth, in the palace of King Creon.

But it was not fated that this couple should have a happy life together. Jason fell in love with Glauce, the daughter of Creon, and determined to marry

Pelias, seated on his throne, receives Jason as he returns to his homeland in triumph. A Nike (Victory) flies towards the hero to crown him. (Apulian krater, 350 - 340 BC).

In this scene we see Medea, in her despair because she has lost the love of Jason, mercilessly knifing one of her children, while he stretches out his hand towards her in supplication, and tries to find sanctuary at the altar and statue of Apollo. (Campanian amphora, c. 330 - 320 BC).

Medea, on the left, pronounces the last magic words, and the ram emerges from the pot rejuvenated. On the right, one of the daughters of Pelias demonstrates her astonishment by her gestures. (Red-figure stamnos, c. 470 BC).

her. In vain did Medea remind him that he had sworn to be eternally faithful to her. Then the king, fearing that Medea would create obstacles to the happiness of his daughter, ordered her to leave the city, together with her children. In her anger, Medea sent Glauce a dress and a crown of pure gold, supposedly as wedding gifts, smeared with a magic unguent. As soon as the unsuspecting girl put them on, she was wrapped in a sheet of flame and met a terrible death, together with her father, who had come to try to save her.

The next victims of Medea's vengeful fury were her own children. Without paying any attention to their tears and pleas, she drew her sword and slaughtered them. Later, she mounted a chariot of fire drawn by winged dragons sent to her by her grandfather the Sun, and flew through the air to Athens, where she married King Aegeus.

Variants of the myth

According to one version of the myth, Medea did not kill her own children to take revenge on Jason, but that they should not fall into the hands of Creon. Others said that she had entrusted them to the sanctuary of Acraea Hera and that the Corinthians themselves had murdered them and blamed their death on her. As to Jason, some said that he was burnt together with Glauce and Creon, or that he hanged himself. According to another view, Medea sent him to sleep below the stern of the Argo, and, because it had rotted, it fell on his head and killed him. The tradition which says that Jason and Medea were reconciled and returned, happy ever after, to Colchis is a later one.

Perseus attacks the sea-monster which was menacing Andromeda. (Caeretan black-figure hydria, attributed to the Eagle Painter, 530 - 520 BC).

On the outer band are depicted the labours of Theseus, and in the centre, in all probability, the hero himself with his friend Pirithous. (Attic red-figure kylix - interior - attributed to the Penthesilea Painter, c. 450 BC).

Perseus

Zeus, transformed into a shower of gold, has entered the underground chamber where the King of Argos, Acrisius, has imprisoned his daughter Danae, and has united himself with her. The fruit of this union between Zeus and Danae was a great hero: Perseus. (Red-figure krater, 490 - 480 BC).

*A*crisius, King of Argos and father of a daughter of the greatest beauty, Danae, decided one day to find out if it would be granted to him to have male children. He therefore sought a pronouncement from the oracle, which told him that though he himself would have no son, his daughter would, and that her son would kill him. Acrisius, fearing that the oracle would prove true, locked Danae up in an underground room and saw to it that no man ever went near here. But he was unable to alter fate. Zeus, delighted by the charms of the girl, decided to make her his, and, transformed into a shower of gold, gained entry to her prison. Thus Danae gave birth to a boy, who took the name of Perseus.

Although Danae attempted to conceal the existence of the baby from her father, his crying betrayed them. When Acrisius demanded to know what exactly had happened, his daughter told him the whole truth, but he did not believe her. En-

In this picture, Acrisius, King of Argos, gives instructions to the carpenter who is constructing the box in which the king is going to shut his daughter Danae and his little grandson Perseus, whom a nurse holds in her arms. (Red-figure hydria, c. 490 BC).

The Gorgons

In the distant West, near the country of the Hesperides, lived the Gorgons, daughters of Phorcys and Ceto: the mortal Medusa or Gorgo and her immortal sisters Stheno and Euryale. The Gorgons were monsters with the hair of snakes, the tusks of a wild boar, bronze hands and gold wings, and were feared and abhorred by all, mortals and immortals alike. In the modern Greek tradition, Gorgona was the sister of Alexander the Great, who laid on her the curse that she should be a fish from the waist downwards, because she had accidently spilled the water of immortality which her brother had taken after killing the dragon which guarded it. From then on, Gorgona travelled about the seas asking seamen if King Alexander still lived. When she received a positive reply she calmed the waves; but if it was negative, she became enraged and sank the ships.

raged, he shut mother and child in a large wooden box and threw it into the sea. Carried by the waves, the box reached Seriphos in the Cyclades, where Dictys, whom some said was an ordinary island fisherman and others that he was the brother of Polydectes, King of Seriphos, found it in his nets.

In the home of Dictys, Danae and Perseus found refuge and were cared for. The only problem was King Polydectes, who wanted to take Danae as his wife, against her will. One day, when Perseus was now a well-grown youth, Polydectes summoned him to his palace, to a banquet which he was holding for his friends. As soon as the young man arrived at the palace, he asked the king for what purpose the banquet was being held, to which he replied 'for horses' - which meant that all the guests had to make a present of a horse to the host, as was the custom in those days. Perseus answered that he would have no objection to giving the king a gift, even if it were the head of Medusa, one of the three Gorgons. The next day, the king accepted with pleasure the horses brought by his friends, but ordered Perseus to bring him the head of Medusa, as he had boasted; and he threatened him that he would marry his mother by force if he did not obey his will.

Perseus and Medusa

The Gorgon Gorgo or Medusa, from the centre of the western pediment of the Temple of Artemis on Corfu, c. 580 BC.

Perseus, with the sickle still in his hand, the magic hat, the winged sandals, and the head of the Medusa in the bag, hastens off to Seriphos, while the decapitated Gorgon is in her death throes on the ground. On the right, Perseus's protectress, Athena, fully-armed, looks on. (Red-figure hydria, c. 460 BC).

Perseus, in despair over the misfortune which had overtaken him, was sitting on a rock when suddenly Hermes presented himself before him and consoled him. He told him that he himself and Athena would help him to take the head of Medusa. Further, he told him that in order to accomplish this great task, he would have to have in his possession a hat which would make him invisible (the hat of darkness), winged sandals, and a magic bag (*kibisis*), items which were kept by the nymphs. The only ones who could lead him to the nymphs were the Graiae, the sisters of the Gorgons.

The Graiae, old women from their birth, had only one eye and one tooth between them. Following the instructions of Athena, Perseus took away their eye and their tooth, and would not give them back unless they showed him the way to the nymphs. The nymphs willingly lent him their valuable equipment, and so the hero, Hermes, and Athena crossed the Ocean and came to the end of the world, where the Gorgons lived. As soon as Athena showed Perseus Medusa, who was at that moment sleeping next to her sisters, he put on the winged sandals and the hat, and, equipped with a sickle of diamonds which Hermes had given him, rushed upon her. If he looked her in the face, he was in danger of turning to stone. For this reason, Athena had advised him to use his shiny shield as a mirror. So Perseus looking at his shield, cut off the head of Medusa and put it into the magic bag. Immediately, Chrysaor, father of the three-bodied Geryones, and Pegasus, the winged horse, fruit of her union with Poseidon, sprang from the severed neck. It is said that as Perseus flew away, some drops of Medusa's

In this scene, Perseus, wearing the magic hat and the winged sandals, looks at the daughter of the King of Ethiopia, Andromeda, who is bound to stakes, as food for the monster. (Krater with a white background, 440 - 435 BC).

The sisters of the Gorgons, the Graiae, were alone able to help Perseus to acquire the means necessary to take the head of the Medusa. In order to blackmail them, he took from them their single eye and tooth, and they promised their help if he would give them back. In this scene, Perseus, below, jumps to snatch the eye which the Graia on the right is giving to her two sisters on the left. Also present, besides Athena and Hermes, is Phorcys, the father of the Graiae and the Gorgons, and Poseidon, Medusa's lover. (Lid of a pyxis, c. 425 BC).

blood fell on Africa, which ever afterwards was full of wild beasts.

On his way back, the hero passed through Ethiopia. There he found a girl tied to a rock. This was Andromeda, daughter of King Cepheus and Cassiope or Cassiepeia. In order to punish her mother, who had boasted that Andromeda was more beautiful than the Nereids, Poseidon sent a flood and a terrible voracious monster to the country. In their fear, the inhabitants asked the oracle how they could escape from the havoc, and the answer which they received was that the only solution was to let the monster devour the king's daughter. Having heard the story, Perseus lay in wait for the monster and killed it, and then married Andromeda.

After these adventures, Perseus returned to Seriphos together with his wife, and there he learnt that Polydectes was pressing Danae to marry him. With no loss of time, he presented himself at the palace, where he took the head of Medusa out of its bag and showed it to the king and his friends, whereupon they were turned to stone.

The end of Acrisius

As soon as Perseus had finished with the evil Polydectes, he went to Argos to meet his grandfather. But Acrisius, who was afraid of the oracle, fled to Larissa, where, however, the hero found him, assured him that he meant him no harm, and persuaded him to return with him to their city. But before they left, Perseus took part in some games and, throwing a quoit, accidently struck his grandfather on the foot and killed him. Since he could not find it in himself to sit on the throne of Acrisius, he agreed with Megapenthes, son of Proetus, the twin-brother of Acrisius, who ruled at Tiryns, that they should exchange kingdoms. Later, Perseus enlarged his power by building the renowned Mycenae.

Cadmus,
founder of Thebes

Cadmus married Harmonia, daughter of the god Ares. In this picture, Cadmus and Harmonia are shown in a chariot drawn by a lion and a boar, at the head of the wedding procession, with Apollo as cithara-player. (Black-figure amphora, early 5th century BC).

When Agenor, King of Phoenicia, discovered that Zeus had abducted his beautiful daughter Europa, he sent his three sons, Phoenix, Cilix, and Cadmus, to find her. The first of these set out to Africa and went as far as Carthage, without any result. The second headed for Asia Minor and, since he did not find his sister either, stayed in a country which was thereafter called Cilicia. The third son, Cadmus, began to wander around Greece. After he had visted various areas, he asked the advice of the oracle of Delphi, which told him that he must now stop looking for Europa and follow a cow which had as a distinguishing mark a white circle, like a full moon, on each of its sides. At a certain place the cow would tire and sit down. There, the oracle advised, he should build a city and settle.

So Cadmus and his men found the cow in a fold, bought it, and let it free. Thus they were led to Boeotia and as soon as they reached what is now Thebes, the cow went down on its knees from weariness. Then Cadmus realised that this was the place of which the oracle had spoken and decided to sacrifice the cow to Athena. So he sent his men to a nearby spiring to fetch water. But the spring was guarded by a snake, the offspring of Ares, and it killed most of Cadmu's men. Enraged, Cadmus confronted the snake on his own, crushed its head with a stone, took water, and offered the sacrifice.

Then, following the advice of Athena, he took out the snake's teeth and sowed them

Cadmus, the founder of Thebes, holding a stone, prepares to kill the dragon, son of the god Ares, which is preventing him from filling his hydria from the spring of Ares. A woman, perhaps Harmonia, sits next to the spring's reed thicket. Athena, protectress of Cadmus, and Ares, father of the dragon, frame the scene. (Red figure krater, c. 450 BC)

in the ground, whereupon armed men sprang up out of the ground, the Sparti (those who have been sown). Terrified, Cadmus threw a stone among them, and they, thinking that one of their number had thrown it, began to fight among themselves until they were all killed except five. The Sparti who survived were the first inhabitants of the new city, which was built on a hill and took the name of Cadmeia. Later, Amphion and Zethus, descendants of the Sparti, walled Cadmeia and built the lower city, which was said to be called Thebes after the wife of Zethus, Theba.

Ares, however, was angered by the killing of the snake, and compelled Cadmus to serve him for eight whole years. As soon as the punishment was completed, the hero became king of the city and married Harmonia, daughter of Ares and Aphrodite. At the wedding, which went down in history for its splendour, the Muses sang and all the gods were present and brought the couple rich gifts. But of all the gifts, the most striking were those given by the bridegroom himself to the bride: a marvellous necklace, the work of Hephaestus, and a garment woven by the kindly Graces.

Cadmus in Illyria

After he had reigned for many years at Thebes, Cadmus took Harmonia and went to Illyria. There lived the Encheleans, who were at war with the Illyrians and who had received an oracle to the effect that they would be victorious only if they appointed Cadmus as their leader - which they did. The Encheleans subjugated the Illyrians, and Cadmus, to whom they owed their victory, became King of Illyria. But the hero had begun to age and, reasoning that the snake which he had killed in his youth was the offspring of a god, sought of the gods that they would change him into a snake. His request was granted; Harmonia too became a snake, and thus they lived, until Zeus sent them to dwell in the Elysian Fields.

The children of Cadmus

When they were living in Thebes, Cadmus and Harmonia had four daughters: Semele, Ino, Agave, and Autonoe, and a single son, Polydorus.

Their first daughter, Semele, was the object of the burning passion of Zeus, and he slept with her. Thus the girl became pregnant with Dionysus, but before she could give birth, she met with a tragic end because of the jealousy of Hera.

The second daughter, Ino, married Athamas, King of Orchomenus, and she too was punished by Hera, because she looked after the baby of her prematurely dead sister. Agave married Echion, one of the Sparti, and gave birth to a son, Pentheus, to whom it was granted to ascend the throne of Thebes. But because she had abused her sister Semele for her relationship with Zeus, Dionysus took a cruel revenge on her. When he had made her and the women of her city the instruments of his orgiastic worship, he went to Thebes to impose this worship there. Pentheus, however, like other kings in other places, was not well disposed towards the new cult, and gave orders that the god should be arrested and imprisoned. But Dionysus not only managed to escape, but also enticed the king out of the city, on the pretence of helping him to spy on the rites of the women. Thus Pentheus fell into the hands of his mother and the other Maenads, who, in their ecstasy, thought that he was a wild beast and tore him apart. It was Agave herself who entered Thebes triumphantly holding the

Dionysus harshly punished the sisters of his mother, Semele, because, in their jealousy, they had spoken ill of her: he sent them mad and, making them take to the mountains, had them establish his orgiastic worship in the open countryside. In the picture, Agave and the other sisters of Semele hold the limbs of Pentheus, son of Agave and King of Thebes, whom they had met on Cithaeron and, in their frenzy, had torn apart. (Red-figure kalpe, c. 500 BC).

head of her son, in the belief that it was a hunting trophy.

The fourth of the sisters, Autonoe, was the wife of Aristaeus, son of Apollo, and mother of Actaeon. As he grew up, Actaeon became a renowned hunter and the companion of Artemis in her wanderings in the forests. One evening, however, the goddess was tired by walking and plunged into a spring on Cithaeron to cool herself. The young man had the misfortune to choose that moment to water his fifty famous hunting dogs and, unintentionally, saw Artemis bathing. In anger, she changed him into a stag and then enraged his beloved dogs, so that they fell upon him and tore him to pieces. Unable to bear the untimely loss of her child, Autonoe fled to the Megarid, where she died.

Polydorus, the only son of Cadmus and Harmonia, succeeded his father on the throne of Thebes. His wife was Nyctyis, daughter of Nycteus, a descendant of the Sparti, who bore him a son, Labdacus, the founder of the great Theban dynasty of the Labdacids.

Amphion and Zethus

Antiope, also a daughter of Nycteus, became pregnant by Zeus. Persecuted for this offence by her father and, later, when Nycteus died, her brother Lycus, she gave birth on Cithaeron to two sons, Amphion and Zethus, whom she was compelled to abandon. Later, her uncle handed her over to his wife, Dirce, who treated her badly. The two brothers, who were brought up by a shepherd, when they learnt who their mother was and what troubles she had, killed Dirce and forced Lycus to hand over to them the rule over Thebes. Although they were twins, Zethus and Amphion had very different interests. The former was a warrior and a hunter, while the latter was a superb musician. It was said, moreover, that when they were building the walls of Cadmeia, the stones went to their places of their own accord, so enchanted were they by his music.

115

Oedipus

*Here we see the meeting
of Oedipus with the
Sphinx, who sits on a high
column, while Oedipus,
wearing the petasos and
sitting on a rock, listens
to her attentively.
(Interior of a red-figure
kylix, 5th century BC).*

Oedipus, the most tragic of all the heroes of Greek mythology, was descended from Cadmus. His father was Laius, son of Labdacus and grandson of Polydorus. When Laius ascended the throne of Thebes, he married Jocasta, daughter of Menoecius and sister of Creon. However, the years passed and the couple had no son. So the king sought an oracle at Delphi. This advised him to remain without an heir, because his own child would kill him, would marry his mother, and would bring upon the city unspeakable disasters. Deeply troubled, Laius avoided Jocasta, but she succeeded in getting him drunk at some celebration and lured him to her bed. As a result, a son was born. At once, Laius had his ankles bored through and his feet bound together with gold links. He then gave orders to a shepherd whom he trusted to abandon him on Cithaeron. But the shepherd felt sorry for the child and gave him to some herders of horses who worked for Polybus, King of Corinth, without telling them who he belonged to. Polybus and his wife, Merope, had no children, so they were glad to take in the infant whom the herders brought them. They called him Oedipus (meaning 'with swollen feet'), because his feet were swollen where Laius had had the links inserted.

Life at the palace of Polybus passed happily enough for Oedipus, until he got into a quarrel with a drunk, who taunted him that he was a bastard. The hero, having tried without success to inveigle the truth from the royal couple, decided to address himself to the oracle. The only thing he learnt, however, was that he would kill his father and marry his mother, and so he continued to think of Polybus and Merope as his real parents.

In order to avoid the prophecy coming true, Oedipus began to wan-

Laius offers sacrifice before the statue of Apollo at Delphi, where he had gone to seek the advice of the god as to how he could have a son. Behind is the slave who accompanies him. (Detail) (Sarcophagus cover, 3rd century AD).

The shepherd who has abandoned the infant Oedipus on Cithaeron in accordance with the instructions of Laius now regrets his action. (Detail) (Sarcophagus cover, 3rd century AD).

The shepherd heads for Cithaeron, holding in his arms the infant Oedipus, who rests his head trustingly on the shepherd's shoulder and places his hand tenderly on his chest. (Red-figure amphora, after 450 BC).

der from place to place. One day, when he was in Phocis, he met with Laius and his entourage at a point where three roads met. When a servant ordered him out of the way so that they could pass, Oedipus refused to move, whereupon Laius ordered the driver of his carriage to start. The horses trod on the feet of Oedipus, who, in a rage, killed the servant and made as if to continue on his way. But as

The riddle of the Sphinx

The question which the Sphinx put to travellers was: what is it which lives on the earth and has two legs and three legs and four legs, and when it goes on three, goes much more slowly?. The answer of Oedipus was man, because when he is a child he goes on all fours, when he grows up he walks on two legs, and when he gets old, he uses a stick as a third leg.

he was passing the carriage, the king struck him with his rod. Even more angry now, Oedipus killed Laius and all his men, apart from one, who hastened back to Thebes, where he put it about that the king had been murdered by robbers.

At that same time, in the region of Thebes, the Sphinx had made its appearance. This was a winged monster with the head of a woman and the body of a lion who stopped passers-by, asked them a riddle and, since none of them could solve it, tore them to pieces. In order to save his city, Creon, who had become king after the death of Laius, proclaimed that he would give his rule and the queen as wife to whoever solved the riddle. The hero, who happened to pass by that way, solved the riddle, and the Sphinx jumped from a rock and was killed. Thus, Oedipus ascended the throne of Thebes and married Jocasta.

Oedipus, King of Thebes

In front of the palace at Thebes, a messenger brings the news to Oedipus and his family that Polybus, King of Corinth, has died; he also tells Oedipus that he is not the real son of Polybus. The tension of the situation is apparent in the scene here. This will reach its climax when, shortly, the whole truth - which will destroy Oedipus and his mother and wife, Jocasta- is revealed. (Sicilian krater, third quarter of the 4th century BC).

From his marriage with Jocasta, Oedipus had four children: two boys, Eteocles and Polynices, and two girls, Antigone and Ismene. All was quiet at Thebes when a terrible plague suddenly broke out which decimated the citizens. Oedipus therefore sent Creon to Delphi, where he was told that if this evil was to stop, the murderer of Laius must be driven out of Thebes. The whole city knew of this oracle, and the king promised that if the guilty person was a citizen and gave himself up of his own accord, he would be let free to depart. Anyone who knew something but concealed it he cursed: such a man would not be able to find shelter and hospitality anywhere and it would be forbidden for him to attend sacrifices.

In spite of these threats and promises, no one came forward who knew who the killer was. So Oedipus summoned the renowned seer Tiresias, who, to begin with, hestitated to reveal the identity of the murderer. But when the king accused him of possible involvement in the murder, the prophet revealed the terrible secret: the man they were looking for was none other than Oedipus. Although the word of Tiresias carried great weight, Oedipus's first thought was that Creon had got him to accuse him so that he could recover his kingdom. Indeed, Oedipus went so far as to voice his suspicions openly and to threaten Creon with death. At this point, Jocasta intervened, providing details of the death of Laius such that Oedipus began to realise that

The shepherd who took Oedipus to Cithaeron now recognises him. (Sarcophagus cover, 3rd century AD).

he was indeed the murderer. However, he did not yet suspect that Laius was his father.

At that moment, a messenger arrived from Corinth to say that Polybus was dead and that the people wished Oedipus to be their king. He, however, replied that he was afraid to go to Corinth, lest the second half of the oracle, which said that he would marry his mother, should come true. In order to reassure him, the messenger told him that he was not the true son of Polybus. This he knew because he himself had taken the baby from the hands of Laius's shepherd, on Cithaeron. In fear and trembling, Oedipus sent for the old shepherd, who lived in the fields, and he confirmed that the infant which he had given to the Corinthian was the child of Laius. Then it was that Oedipus realised that he had killed his father and married his mother. As soon as the truth came to light, Jocasta rushed to her room, shut herself in, and hanged herself. Oedipus, unable now to look the world in the face, took the brooches from her dress, stuck them into his eyes, and blinded himself with his own hand.

The seer Tiresias

Tiresias was the son of Eueres, a descendant of the Sparti, and the nymph Chariclo. One day he saw two snakes copulating and struck them with his rod; immediately he was transformed into a woman. Seven years later, he chanced to see the snakes again, struck them, and became a man again. For this reason, when Zeus and Hera happened to disagree about who feels the greater pleasure in love-making, the man or the woman, they asked Tiresias, who had lived as a member of both sexes. He replied that if erotic satisfaction has ten parts, nine of them are enjoyed by the woman and only one by the man. This made Hera angry, because she had maintained that the man has the greater pleasure, and she blinded him. Then Zeus gave him, as recompense, the gift of prophecy and allowed him to live for seven generations.

Oedipus at Colonus

*O*edipus, who had once saved Thebes by his wisdom, now left its gates blind and despised, his

only companion his daughter Antigone. Since his misfortunes had become widely know, and everyone thought him accursed, he was driven out from everywhere he went. Finally, he found his way to Colonus in Attica, where he invoked the hospitality of Athens and sought to speak to King Theseus, saying that his presence there would be beneficial for the city.

In the meantime, Ismene arrived at Colonus bearing bad news from the palace: after the flight of Oedipus, his two sons had each laid claim to the throne of Thebes for himself, and the younger, Eteocles, had driven his brother Polynices from the city. He had taken refuge in Argos, where he had married the daughter of King Adrastus, Argeia. With the aid of Adrastus and his friend Tydeus, Polynices had organised the famous expedition of the Seven against Thebes, so called because the army was led by seven brave warrior-chiefs, and had set out to capture Thebes.

At the same time, an oracle had become known which said that the party which had Oedipus on its side would win. For that reason, Creon was coming to Athens to persuade him to return to his city; but since he was a parricide, they would not allow him to enter the city, but would keep him outside the walls, just so that the oracle would come true. So when Creon arrived, Oedipus, warned by Ismene,

Tydeus

Tydeus was the son of Oeneus, king of Calydon in Aetolia, by his second wife, Periboea. As a young man, he had been exiled by his father because he had accidentally killed a relative, possibly Toxeus, son of Oeneus and Althaea. This was why he was living at the palace of Adrastus, King of Argos. There he met Polynices and in the night they began to fight like wild beasts about who should have which sleeping quarters. They were parted by Adrastus and after that the two men became inseparable friends. Tydeus, moreover, married Deipyle, the sister of Argeia. By this marriage Tydeus had a son, Diomedes, who was to outdo his father in reputation and bravery.

Adrastus, King of Argos, has organised a major expedition against Thebes, to restore his son-in-law Polynices to its throne, of which he has been deprived by his brother Eteocles. Ferocious warlords, pictured here, were put at the head of the army. (Red-figure kalpe, c. 470 BC).

treated him with obvious hostility and refused to agree to his proposals. Then Creon planned to abduct Ismene and Antigone, in order to blackmail Oedipus into coming with him, but Theseus interposed and made him abandon his plan, as being a slight on the laws of hospitality.

A little later, Polynices arrived to seek the help of his father. But Oedipus, who regarded his two sons as being responsible for his exile and his hardships, because they had not defended him and honoured him as they should, laid a curse upon him that he should never rule Thebes but would drown in blood, both he and his brother. A little later, the old king felt that his end was approaching. He then imparted to Theseus a secret which was to be passed from father to son and would protect Athens from any attack by Thebes. After this, he asked everyone to leave him, except for Theseus, and then, in a mysterious way, he disappeared from the face of the earth.

Antigone and Ismene

A selection of key episodes from the deadly war of the 'Seven against Thebes' is pictured here. On the left Oedipus, Jocasta and Antigone attempt to calm the two brothers Eteocles and Polynices, who are preparing to attack one another. Nearby, Capaneus climbs a ladder to the battlements of the wall. Further to the right, Amphiaraus in his chariot disappears into a chasm, from which Ge (?) emerges, while the corpses of three warriors lie above him. Further off, Eteocles and Polynices knife each other, and on the extreme right Antigone and Argeia remove the dead Polynices from the field of battle, while the men set to guard the body sleep on unawares. (Sarcophagus, late 2nd century AD).

The Seven against Thebes expedition had in the end the most tragic outcome. Eteocles and Polynices fell dead, killed by one another, before the walls of Thebes, and then the defenders crushed the besiegers. The seven proud generals were all killed, with the exception of Adrastus, who managed to escape thanks to his divine horse, Arion, the child of Demeter and Poseidon. But the defenders of Cadmeia, the acropolis of Thebes, had so many losses that from then on any victory which looked more like a defeat was termed a Cadmeian victory.

After the death of the two brothers and the saving of Thebes, Creon ordered that Eteocles and his warriors should be given an honourable burial. But Polynices he dubbed a traitor and gave orders that his body should be left outside the city bounds, to be eaten by birds of prey and dogs. That evening, Antigone, who could not bear to leave one of her two dead brothers naked and despised in the dust, secretly gave Polynices burial, after she had washed and decked him.

As soon as Creon heard that Antigone had disobeyed his orders, he buried her alive in a cellar, dug up the corpse of Polynices and had it thrown where it had initially been left. At that point, Tiresias arrived, deeply disturbed, and told the king that the birds were uttering strange cries, that the offerings to the gods would not burn properly, and that the birds of prey which had touched the body of the son of Oedipus were letting fall from on high drops of blood which fell on the altars and defiled them. Creon, alarmed by the signs from the gods, decided to permit the burial of Polynices and set Antigone free. But in the meantime the girl had hanged herself with a sheet in her prison. Her intended husband, Haemon, the son of Creon, had killed himself with his sword, on top of her dead body.

Equally tragic was the end of Antigone's younger sister, Ismene. During the siege

Shown in this scene are two of the most horrifying episodes fom the Theban War. The most terrible of the seven warlords, Tydeus, has fallen to the ground, and, filled with savage hatred for his great enemy Melanippus, he has broken his skull and is sucking out his brains with insane pleasure. On the left, Athena, holding the vessel of immortality which she has brought from Olympus for her protegé Tydeus, stands frozen with horror at his appalling act. Above the two heroes, Zeus (?) hurls his thunderbolt at Capaneus, who is open-mouth with surprise and terror.
(Earthernware relief from the pediment of Temple A at Pyrgi, second quarter of the 5th century BC).

of Thebes, Tydeus, the most savage of the warriors in the army of the Argives, found the girl in the temple of Athena, together with her beloved, Periclymenus. Periclymenus ran away and managed to escape, but Ismene fell into the hands of Tydeus, who slaughtered her. It is said that Tydeus was led to the spot where the couple were by Athena herself, as she was angered by the fact that the young couple had arranged a lovers' meeting in her temple, or she was moved by hate for Periclymenus, who was the son of Poseidon, her great enemy.

The second expedition against Thebes

Ten years after the fall of the Seven, their sons, who had now grown up, decided to avenge the death of their fathers and to mount a fresh expedition against Thebes. Among the young warriors were Diomedes, son of Tydeus, Aegialeus, son of Adrastus, and Thersander, son of Polynices, who lived at Argos because Thebes was ruled by Laodamas, son of Eteocles. This time things went well for the besiegers. They succeeded in entering the city as victors and with very few losses. The only one who was killed in the battle was the son of Adrastus, Aegialeus.

Tydeus kills Ismene, who emerges half-naked from under the bed cover, while her fiancé, Periclymenus, taken by surprise, has already deserted her.
(Corinthian amphora, c. 560 BC).

Bellerophon

The scene here shows the hero Bellerophon riding on Pegasus, the winged horse given to him by his father, Poseidon, and aiming his spear from on high at the Chimaera, the daughter of Typhon and Echidna, a terrible monster with the body and head of a lion, a head with the neck of a goat sprouting from her back, and a snake for a tail. (Italiotic tablet, second half of the 4th century BC)

*B*ellerophon, the great hero of Corinth, was thought to be the son of Glaucus and the grandson of Sisyphus, but in reality his father was Poseidon. His mother was Eurynome or Eurymede, daughter of Nisus of Megara. At the time when Corinth was ruled by Bellerophon, the city was subject to Argos. At some point, Antea, wife of the King of Argos, Proetus, saw the hero and fell in love with him for his beauty and manliness, but he, not wishing to offend the king, declined her advances. So Antea, either to take revenge or because she feared that he would betray her to her husband, accused him of attempting to make her his against her will. Proetus, believing the words of his wife, decided to punish Bellerophon. However, as he did not wish to defile his hands with the blood of a guest, he sent him to Lycia, to his father-in-law, Iobates, supposedly to deliver some important message. So the hero set out for Lycia, bearing a sealed tablet, on which Proetus had written to Iobates that he was to kill the bearer.

For nine days Ibates entertained the emissary, and it was only on the tenth that he asked the purpose of his visit. Unsuspecting, Bellerophon handed over the missive, and Iobates, as soon as he had read it, decided to set him impossible tasks, certain that he would be killed in that way. First of all, he asked him to deal with the Chimaera, the daughter of Typhon and Echidna, a fierce monster with the head of a lion, the body of a goat, and the tail of a snake, which was devouring the animals of the inhabitants of Lycia. Immediately the hero mounted Pegasus, the winged horse which had been given to him by his father, Poseidon, and killed

The Corinthian hero Bellerophon was once a guest at the palace of the King of Argos Proetus. While he was staying at the palace, Stheneboea (or Antea), wife of Proetus, fell in love with the handsome youth. But, meeting with no response, she accused him to her husband that he had attempted to seduce her. Proetus in his anger sent Bellerophon to his father-in-law, Iobates, King of Lycia, with a letter telling him to put the young man to death. It is this scene which is shown here. Bellerophon, holding Pegasus, who will carry him to Lycia, by the rein, unsuspectingly takes the letter containing his death sentence from Proetus, who, together with his wife, bids him farewell. (Lucanian amphora, c. 410 BC).

In this scene, the two deities of Hades, with their symbols, Pluto with his sceptre and Persephone with her ears of corn, watch the torment to which Sisyphus, in Hades for the second time, has been condemned: to push a huge rock up a steep hill. But the rock never reached the top; instead it slipped from his hands and rolled back to the bottom, where the hero had to start again from the beginning. This torment was repeated endlessly. (Black-figure amphora, 510 - 500 BC).

the Chimaera, shooting an arrow at it from on high. His second mission was to fight the Solymi, a savage people of Lycia, enemies of Iobates; when he defeated them, he was ordered to mount an expedition into the country of the Amazons. When he returned victorious from this battle also, Bellerophon fell into an ambush laid for him by the bravest warriors of Lycia, on the orders of Iobates. It was only when he wiped out the Lycians that Iobates realised that he must have been of divine origin.

After all this, the king kept Bellerophon with himself, married him to his second daughter, who some say was called Cassandra, and shared his power with him. But the hero came to a bad end. In his arrogance, he attempted with his winged horse to ascend Olympus and join the gods at table, but Pegasus threw him off and he fell to earth. From then on, Bellerophon wandered in solitude, having taken leave of his senses, driven out by gods and men.

Sisyphus

Sisyphus, son of Aeolus, was famed for his great cunning. One day, when he had revealed to the River Asopus that Zeus had abducted his daughter Aegina, the god decided to punish him by sending him to Hades. But he succeeded in tricking Thanatos (Death) and binding him in chains. Finally, Thanatos was released by Ares and seized Sisyphus, who, before he died, gave orders to his wife not to pay him the usual honours. When he arrived in the Underworld, he presented himself before Persephone and asked permission to return to earth to punish his wife for this omission. Persephone agreed, and the wily king left, naturally with no intention of returning. However, when Sisyphus did go down to Hades for good, he paid for his misdoings by eternal suffering.

Meleager and the hunting of the Calydonian Boar

Meleager gathered together from all over Greece a host of men and dogs to deal with the huge boar which Artemis had sent as a punishment to Calydon in Aetolia and which was laying waste the royal estates. In this detail three pairs of hunters are attacking the boar, which is already pierced with arrows: from the left, Atalanta and Melanion, Meleager and Peleus, and from the right, Castor and Pollux. Another hero, Angaeus - according to the inscription, Antaeus - lies mortally wounded. Also dead is the hound Hormenus, with its belly ripped open. The hound Marpsas can just be seen on the back of the boar; Corax is biting it from the rear, while Egertes attacks menacingly from the right, and Methepon from the left. (Black-figure krater, known as the François Vase, c. 570 BC).

C alydon in Aetolia was once ruled by Oeneus, who had married Althaea, daughter of Thestius, King of neighbouring Pleuron. One summer, when Oeneus offered to the gods the first-fruits produced by the earth, he forgot to sacrifice to Artemis, the country's protector. This angered the goddess, and she sent a huge boar, which wrought havoc on the royal estates. So Meleager, the son of Oeneus, called together a host of heroes from all over Greece, among them his uncle, the brother of Althaea and leader of the Curetes, who lived at Pleuron, to hunt the Calydonian Boar.

The task was a hard one, and many brave warriors died, torn by the beast's fearful tusks. But eventually Meleager succeeded in killing it, after his uncle had seriously injured it. As the hero's bad luck would have it, Artemis again intervened by making him quarrel with the brother of Althaea as to who should take home the skin of the boar as a trophy. Soon the quarrel developed into a real battle between the Aetolians and the Curetes, and Meleager, either by accident or in a duel, killed his uncle. As soon as Althaea heard of the death of her brother, she asked the gods of the Underworld to take her son to themselves.

Meleager, in his turn, hearing of his mother's words, obstinately withdrew from the battle. Thus, the Curetes, emboldened by the absence of the bravest warrior on the other side, began to besiege the walls of Calydon. As the city was in danger of falling into their hands, all its inhabitants, even Althaea herself, attempted to assuage the hero's anger, but he could not be talked round. Finally, the situation was saved by his wife, Cleopatra, who with tears in her eyes told of the sufferings which await a city which is taken by its enemies. Moved by her words, Meleager returned to the battle, drove out the Curetes, and saved his country. But

Meleager quarrelled with the brother of his mother, Althaea, as to who was to take home the skin of the boar as a trophy, and, either accidentally or in a duel, killed him. Althaea, angered by the death of her brother, asked the gods of the Underworld to take her son to themselves. In the picture, Tydeus is attempting, together with Deianeira, to put Meleager on his bed so that he can die. A woman, probably Althaea, enters in distress from the left, perhaps regretting her action. (Apulian krater, 375 - 350 BC).

Meleager, in love with Atalanta, who had so distinguished herself in the hunting of the boar, gives her its skin. Aphrodite watches on the left, while Eros hovers between them. (Apulian amphora, c. 330 BC).

he did not live to enjoy the victory. The curse of Althaea had already reached the ears of the gods of the Underworld.

According to tradition, among those who took part in the hunting of the Calydonian Boar were many courageous men, such as Peleus, Acastus, Admetus, Jason, Mopsus, Pirithous, Castor, Pollux, Iphicles, or his son Iolaus, Theseus, Telamon - and a woman, Atalanta. When Atalanta was born, her father, who had wanted a son, left her in some mountain region of Arcadia to die. But she was fed there by a bear, before being found by some hunters who brought her up. Atalanta, brought up in the mountains, was invincible in running, wrestling, and archery. A variant form of the myth, contained in Euripides, says that Atalanta was first to wound the boar, and that Meleager finished it off and, because he had fallen in love with this beautiful girl, gave her its skin. The other hunters, indignant because the trophy had gone to a woman, rushed upon her and took it away from her by force. When she complained of this to Meleager, he in his anger killed his uncles, which led to his own death.

In this vase-painting, a section of a crowded composition has been highlighted. Two hunters, very probably Meleager and Atalanta, the chief figures in the undertaking, charge with javelins against the boar. (Interior of a Laconian kylix, c. 550 BC).

The discovery of wine

One day, a shepherd of King Oeneus, Staphylus, noticed that one of his goats, which was eating the fruit of an unknown plant, seemed more lively than the others. Puzzled, he brought this fruit to the king, who pressed it, tried the juice, and immediately felt rejuvenated. Thus he called the fruit *staphyle* (= grapes) after Staphylus, and the juice *oinos* (= wine), after himself.

127

Pelops

Pelops, in the chariot with Hippodamia, skilfully drives the horses which will bring him victory. Hippodamia raises her hand in surprise as she sees before her the two doves sent by Aphrodite as a divine sign that she will become the partner of the youth who is at her side. (Red-figure amphora, c. 410 BC).

*T*antalus, son of Zeus and King of Lydia, to thank the gods for having been deemed worthy to ascend to Olympus and taste of ambrosia and nectar, decided to invite them to dinner. But wishing to put them to the test, he slaughtered Pelops, his son by Dione, daughter of Atlas, had him cooked, and served him as dinner. The gods, who realised at once what Tantalus had done, ordered him to be tortured by eternal hunger and thirst in Hades, and brought Pelops back to life.

In those years, Oenomaus, son of Ares, ruled at Elis and Pisa. He had once received an oracle that the marriage of his only daughter, Hippodamia, would mean the end of his life. So he made a proclamation that he would marry Hippodamia only to the person who was the winner in a chariot race. A necessary condition was that the suitors should take the girl with them in the chariot. As their attention was taken up with her, they were easy prey for her father. Moreover, Oenomaus possessed certain gifts from his father, Ares: invincible weapons and two immortal horses, which ran more swiftly than the wind. Thanks to the skill of his charioteer, Myrtilus, the king, though starting out after the young men, always managed to overtake them and kill them.

The last candidate to present himself was Pelops, who had fallen in love with Hippodamia, while she returned his feelings. In order to ensure the assistance of Myrtilus, the hero promised him that if he won, he would give him half the kingdom and would allow him to enjoy one night with Hippodamia. The charioteer, who entertained a secret passion for the girl, agreed to help. He took out the pins which held

When Pelops realised that it was only with divine help that he would be able to conquer Oenomaus, he went to the sea-shore and implored the assistance of Poseidon. The god heard him and gave him a golden chariot and tireless winged horses which ran as swiftly as the wind. Here Poseidon rises majestically from the sea, mounted on a sea-horse, to answer the prayer of Pelops. (Red-figure hydria, after 400 BC).

on the wheels of Oenomaus's chariot and re-place them with replicas made of wax. So when the chariot race began, the wax melted, and the king became entangled in the reins, was trampled underfoot by the horses, and was killed. A little before he expired, howev-er, he put a curse on Myrtilus that he should die by the hand of Pelops.

The curse of Oenomaus was quick to act. Myrtilus, seething with desire for Hippodamia, attempted to ravish her, whereupon Pelops, who was seeking a chance to get rid of him so that he would not reveal the trick, threw him into the sea. Myrtilus, however, was the son of Hermes, and so it was, they said, that the god was angered and never left the family of Pelops without torments. After the murder of Myrtilus, Pelops was purified by the god Hephaestus and became King of Pisa. Later, he became lord of all the country below the Isthmus of Corinth, which thus took his name and became the Peloponnese.

> ### The children of Pelops
>
> Pelops had many children, among them Atreus, Thyestes, Pittheus, grandfather of Theseus, Nicippe, mother of Eurystheus - and a bastard son, Chrysippus, for whom he had a special weakness. When Atreus and Thyestes killed Chrysippus, because they were afraid that he would be his father's heir, Pelops drove them out of Elis, and so they came to Triphyllia, where Thyestes took the rule out of the hands of Atreus by trickery. Zeus, who would not tolerate injustices, advised Atreus to make a wager with Thyestes that the next day the sun would rise in the west. Whoever won would take the kingdom. Thus Atreus became king, because Zeus made the sun change its course. Later, however, Atreus was killed by Aegisthus, son of Thyestes. The sons of the dead king, Agamemnon and Menelaus, were then forced to flee the country.

In this picture, Tantalus is shown in the Underworld, attempting -according to one version of the myth- to hold off the rock which hangs menacingly over him and eternally torments his soul, as a punishment of the gods for the irreverence which he showed towards them. (Apulian krater, late 4th century BC).

129

The Trojan War
The Trojan War
The Trojan War

The Trojan War

*I*n very ancient times, a prince of Troy, Paris, abducted the Queen of Sparta, Helen, a woman famous for her beauty. In order to take their revenge, the Achaeans gathered together an army, took to their ships, and set out for Troy. During the ten, seemingly endless, years in which the Achaeans fought the Trojans, many men on both sides lost their lives, some with honour and others ingloriously. In the end, Troy was taken by cunning and completely destroyed.

In the post-Mycenaean period, many important epic poets took the myths of Troy as their subject. In the second half of the 8th century BC, however, Homer took them into his hands and in his epic work of genius, the Iliad, gave them a new dimension, vigour, and form. Taking as his starting-point and the kernel of his narrative the wrath of Achilles, Homer succeeds in unfolding before our eyes all the events in the ten-year struggle between the Achaeans and Trojans, in a work imbued with unique technical skill.

Until about a hundred years ago, scholarship regarded the Greek myths as purely the product of the imagination. This was until 1871, when an archaeological miracle took place. The amateur archaeologist Heinrich Schliemann, who believed unshakeably that Homer was describing a real war, decided to dig near what is now the village of Hisarlik in Turkey in order to find the city of Troy. Not only did he find Troy, but it is also thanks to his excavations at Mycenae, Tiryns and Orchomenus that

Paris leads Helen to his ship; she follows hesitantly. Behind her, Aphrodite covers her with the bridal veil, while in front Eros arranges her diadem. On the extreme right of the picture is Peitho, and on the left Aeneas, son of Aphrodite. (Red-figure skyphos, c. 480 BC).

Mycenaean civilisation - unknown up till then - was brought to light. So many treasures were found in these digs that it was proved that Homer's descriptions of 'Mycenae rich in gold' and 'the city of Priam rich in gold and bronze' corresponded completely with the reality.

However, the existence of the fortresses of Mycenae and Troy does not necessarily mean that the war between their kings was a historical event, or that Achilles, Hector, and Odysseus were real people. The relation between Greek myth and history is a subject of debate among specialists, who up till now have not managed to reach agreement. Some maintain that myth is a trustworthy source for history, others deny that it has the slightest historical nucleus, and others again hold a position somewhere between these two views.

Studies of more modern heroic poetry of other nations have reached the conclusion that the folk imagination, when it sings of some specific event, does not hesitate to incorporate a host of folk tales and poetic themes gathered from different areas and eras, to represent figures who lived at a distance of two, three, or even five hundred years from the events as friends or opponents on the field of battle, or to turn the actual victors into the vanquished. This is probably what happened in the case of the Trojan War. The starting-point for the weaving of the myths of Troy was perhaps provided by some actual event. But when exactly that event occurred, under what conditions and with what outcome are enigmas which we shall probably never solve.

In this scene the Trojan Horse is shown as enormous, with wheels and a row of apertures. Seven Achaeans can be seen inside it, some of whom have put their hands, holding their weapons, out of the 'windows'. Seven other warriors, Achaeans or Trojans, stand outside the horse.
(Amphora with scenes in relief, c. 670 BC).

The marriage of **Peleus** and **Thetis**

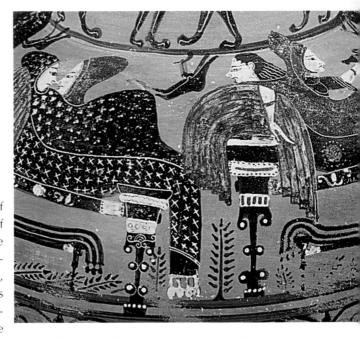

Aeacus, son of Zeus and King of Aegina, had three sons: Peleus and Telamon by his wife, Endeis, and Phocus by the Nereid Psamathe. The three brothers often trained together, but since Phocus always came first in any match, the other two were jealous of him. So one day they killed him and hid his body in the woods. When the murder was discovered, Aeacus drove the fratricides out of Aegina. Telamon took refuge at Salamis and Peleus at Phthia in Thessaly, where he later became king.

Peleus, though a mortal, was deemed worthy to marry a goddess, the nymph Thetis. It is said that once Zeus had quarrelled with Poseidon over the love of Thetis. But when Themis revealed to them that Thetis was fated to give birth to a son who would become more powerful than his father, the two gods, fearing that this child might rob them of their rule over the world, decided to marry her to a mortal. This honour fell to Peleus, who was reputed to be the most god-fearing man in Thessaly.

The marriage of Peleus with Thetis was celebrated with great magnificence on Mt Pelion. The gods descended from Olympus, each with his gifts, while the entertainment was provided by the Muses, accompanied by Apollo himself. The only goddess not to be invited was Eris ('Strife'), who, by way of revenge, threw into the middle of the assembly an apple, saying that it was to be given to the fairest. When

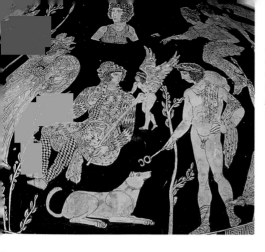

In the landscape of Mt Ida, Hermes presents the three goddesses to Paris, for him to resolve the dispute between them. Eris, in the centre of the composition, is half-hidden. Zeus is also present, as is the personification of happiness (top right). (Red-figure hydria, 400 - 390 BC).

Zeus, according to one version of the myth, consulted Themis on how he should reduce the number of mankind, who were burdening the earth. Themis, seated on the 'navel of the earth' at Delphi, gestures as she talks to Zeus, while Hermes and Aphrodite watch attentively, and Selene (the Moon), on the right, departs on horseback. (Red-figure pelike, 350 - 340 BC).

Hera, Athena and Aphrodite began to vie for this title, Zeus ordered Hermes to take the goddesses to Mt Ida, where Paris, the son of Priam, King of Troy, was grazing his flocks. He would judge which of the three deserved to win the beauty prize.

As soon as Paris saw the goddesses before him, he was deeply perplexed and wanted to run away, but Hermes stopped him and told him of the command of Zeus. So Paris was forced to resolve the dispute. In order to bribe him, each of the goddesses offered him a different gift. Hera told him that if his vote went to her, she would make him ruler of the whole of Asia and Europe, Athena that she would make him an invincible warrior, and Aphrodite that she would give him the most beautiful woman in the world - who was none other than Helen. Without much further thought, Paris chose the offer of Aphrodite and gave her the apple. The first step leading to the outbreak of the Trojan War had been taken.

In this picture, Paris sits on a rock with his lyre in his hand, while Hermes brings before him the three goddesses, divinely beautiful. Athena is shown with her helmet and spear, Hera with her sceptre, and Aphrodite with a flight of winged Eroses surrounding her. (Red-figure kylix, 500 - 490 BC).

The cause of the evil

Once, when mankind had multiplied and were a burden to the earth, Zeus stirred up the Theban War, in which large numbers were killed. But soon mankind had multiplied again and Zeus sought the advice of Momus, son of Nyx ('Night'). He proposed two things: that Zeus should father a daughter of the greatest beauty, and should marry the Nereid Thetis to a mortal. So Zeus became the father of Helen and saw to it that Thetis was married to Peleus. These two happenings led to the Trojan War, in which innumerable mortals lost their lives and the earth was again relieved of its burden. According to another version of the story, the one who advised Zeus how mortals should be decimated was the Titan Themis.

Helen

Helen, the beautiful daughter of Zeus by Leda, was the cause of the most destructive of all the wars in ancient myth - the War of Troy. (Detail). (Black-figure amphora, c. 540 BC)

*O*ne day, Leda, daughter of Thestius, King of Pleuron, and wife of the Spartan King Tyndareus, was bathing in the waters of the River Eurotas when, suddenly, a swan which was being chased by an eagle sought, in its terror, refuge in her arms. The eagle was none other than Hermes and the swan was Zeus himself, who had employed this subterfuge in order to unite himself with her. The same night Leda slept with her husband and so, some months later, gave birth to Helen and to twin boys, Castor and Pollux. Helen and Pollux were the immortal children of Zeus, while the mortal Castor was the son of Tyndareus.

In this picture, Tyndareus, Leda and the Dioscuri are looking at the egg from which, in one version of the myth, Helen emerged, which has been placed on an altar. The statue of Zeus stands on a high column. (Red-figure krater, c. 420 BC).

When Helen was twelve years old, Theseus, beguiled by her beauty, abducted her and shut her in fortified Aphidna. But her brothers, Castor and Pollux, have fought hard against Aphidnus, the local hero and defender of the fortress, managed to rescue her. After the experience of Aphidna, Tyndareus decided to find Helen a husband. Since her beauty had become known throughout the length and breadth of Greece, the most powerful rulers, who vied with each other in wealth and power, presented themselves at Sparta. Only Odysseus, King of Ithaca, failed to make an appearance, but he sent messages from his island to Helen's brothers. Tyndareus now found himself in a very difficult position; he realised that whoever his daughter chose, she would make enemies of all the rest. So, following the advice of Odysseus - according to one version - he made all the suitors swear that if at any time any-

Zeus welcomes to his palaces on Olympus the Dioscuri, who after their earthly life were deified. Poseidon and Ares follow them as a kind of escort of honour.
(Black-figure amphora, 550 - 540 BC).

According to the commonest version of the myth, Zeus gained access to Leda in the guise of a swan and fathered by her Pollux and Helen on the same day that Leda conceived Castor by her mortal husband, Tyndareus. (Roman copy of an original statue by the sculptor Timotheus, c. 370 BC)

one dared to steal Helen from her husband, they would all hasten to punish that person. They willingly swore this oath, without imagining for one moment where this would one day lead them.

The husband whom Helen finally chose was Menelaus, son of Atreus and brother of Agamemnon, by whom she had a daughter, Hermione. Ten years after their marriage, Paris, led by Aphrodite, came to Sparta, seeking 'the wonder among women'. For nine days Menelaus entertained his distinguished guest, but on the tenth he was forced to go to Crete for the funeral of his maternal grandfather, Catreus. The absence of the king assisted the schemes of Aphrodite. Like an ordinary mortal, Helen succumbed to the power of the goddess and fell into the embrace of Paris. By night she loaded the ship of the young prince with treasure and slaves and abandoned the palace and her daughter.

The Dioscuri

The twins Castor and Pollux (known as the Dioscuri = sons of Zeus) met the end of their earthly life when they came into conflict with their cousins Idas and Lynceus, sons of Aphareus, King of Messenia. The cause, as the story goes, was that the Dioscuri had abducted Phoebe and Hilaeira, daughters of Leucippus, brother of Aphareus, who were betrothed to Idas and Lynceus. In the battle which followed, Castor was killed first, by the spear of Idas, and then Lynceus was slain by the spear of Pollux and Idas by a thunderbolt of Zeus. Then Zeus, acceding to the request of the immortal Pollux, who did not wish to be separated from his mortal brother, allowed the Dioscuri to live together, one day on Olympus with the gods and the next on earth. Later, they were honoured as gods and ascended into the heavens where they formed the constellation of the Twins.

The Mobilization

Menelaus and Odysseus, shown here, were responsible for the recruitment for the Trojan campaign. Achilles and Patroclus, before following them, say farewell to Thetis. On the extreme left is Menestheus, leader of the Athenian expeditionary force which went to Troy. The Athenian painter wished to emphasise his presence, and has written the equivalent of 'Here he is!' after his name. (Black-figure kantharos, c. 550 BC).

*A*fter the flight of Paris and Helen, Menelaus, warned of this by Iris, returned to Sparta and saw what had befallen him. In despair, he hastened to Mycenae, where his brother Agamemnon ruled as king and asked him to gather the rulers together to recover Helen, as they had sworn. So Agamemnon sent heralds and gave notice that they should prepare for the campaign. All of them readily responded to the summons, and at the same time Menelaus and Nestor, King of Pylos, made journeys to recruit two heroes who had not been bound by the oath: Odysseus and Achilles (who had been only a boy at the time of Helen's marriage).

On their journey to Ithaca, where Odysseus ruled, Menelaus and Nestor were accompanied by Palamides, son of Nauplius, who was famed for his inventiveness. When they arrived on Ithaca, the three companions found that Odysseus had yoked to his plough a horse and an ox, was wearing on his head a cap like that of Hephaestus, and was sowing salt in the furrow instead of seed. The hero had decided to pretend to be mad, since he had received an oracle which said that if he took part in the war, he would not return to his homeland for twenty years. But Palamides saw through his cunning, and, snatching up Odysseus's wife, Penelope, and his new-born son Telemachus, he laid them on the ground in front of the plough. Naturally, Odysseus at once halted the animals. Thus he gave himself away and was forced to promise Menelaus that he would take part in the campaign.

Achilles was the precious only son of Peleus and Thetis. As soon as he was born, his mother, wishing to give him the gift of immortality, secretly held him in the fire at night. One night, however, Peleus saw her, and in his terror took the child from her hands, and

Achilles, in women's clothing, is recognised by Odysseus and one of his companions in the courtyard of the King of Skyros, Lycomedes, where he had been hidden by his mother, Thetis, to prevent him from taking part in the Trojan War, from which - being a goddess - she knew he would never return. (Wall-painting from the 'House of the Dioscuri' at Pompeii, c. 70 AD).

Menelaus and the other Achaean leaders, before setting out for Troy, stand one after the other in this scene. Distinguished from the crowd, they are great in their merits and their passions. (Drawing of a scene from a hypokraterion, before 650 BC).

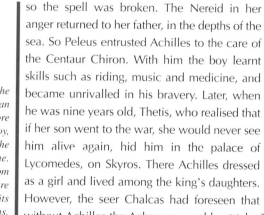

so the spell was broken. The Nereid in her anger returned to her father, in the depths of the sea. So Peleus entrusted Achilles to the care of the Centaur Chiron. With him the boy learnt skills such as riding, music and medicine, and became unrivalled in his bravery. Later, when he was nine years old, Thetis, who realised that if her son went to the war, she would never see him alive again, hid him in the palace of Lycomedes, on Skyros. There Achilles dressed as a girl and lived among the king's daughters. However, the seer Chalcas had foreseen that without Achilles the Achaeans would not take Troy. It was, therefore, essential that the hero should be found. When the emissaries of the Achaeans presented themselves to Lycomedes, he denied that Achilles was in the palace. Then Odysseus disguised himself as a merchant and entered the women's quarters to show the king's daughters the woven materials which he was supposedly selling. In the meantime he had hidden a shield and a sword among the merchandise. While the king's daughters were choosing materials, Achilles, suddenly seeing the weapons, could not restrain himself from seizing them, thus giving away his identity. Later, he promised that he would lead the warriors of Phthia, the Myrmidons, to Troy. Aulis in Boeotia was chosen as the meeting-place for the forces of the Achaeans. There the kings, with their armies and their ships, began to arrive one by one.

Deidamia

While Achilles was living on Skyros, he fell in love with one of the daughters of Lycomedes, Deidamia, and had a son by her - Neoptolemus. According to another version of the story, however, Achilles did not grow up in the palace of the King of Skyros. It was as he was returning from the unsuccessful campaign in Mysia that a storm drove him one night on to the island, and it was then that he met Deidamia and married her.

The
Achaeans

The leader of the Achaeans who took part in the Trojan War was, because of the large military force which he contributed, Agamemnon, shown here pouring a libation in front of the funeral pyre of Patroclus. Detail. (Apulian krater, 340 - 330 BC).

Homer describes Menelaus, younger brother of Agamemnon and King of Sparta, as a brave and good-hearted man. (Red-figure krater, 440 - 430 BC).

*T*he body of the Greeks who took part in the Trojan War are called by Homer and the other epic poets Achaeans, but also Argives and Danaeans. The leader, because of the size of the military force which he contributed, was Agamemnon, son of Atreus. Agamemnon had married Clytemnestra, the sister of Helen, and with the help of his father-in-law, Tyndareus, had recovered the throne of Mycenae, which had been seized by Thyestes, his father's brother. His kingdom extended over the whole of Argos and many islands, but we do not know whether by the geographical term 'Argos' Homer means the city of that name, the Argolid, or the whole of the Peloponnese. The commander-in-chief of the Achaeans, though not particularly renowned for his bravery, is represented as exceeding all the other kings in good looks and nobility.

Menelaus, younger brother of Agamemnon, was King of Sparta and was famed for his wealth. Apart from Hermione, his daughter by Helen, the hero had a son by a slave-girl whom he had named Megapenthes ('great grief'), to remind him of the sorrow which he had felt when his wife left him. The Iliad portrays Menelaus as fair-haired, with broad shoulders, a man of few words, wise and excessively good-hearted.

Nestor, the old and wise King of Pylos, was the son of Neleus, son of Poseidon. He did not take part in battle frequently, but he was respected and honoured by all the Achaeans. Nestor's courage had been inherited by his two sons, Antilochus and Thrasymedes.

Odysseus, the brave King of Ithaca, was renowned above all for his

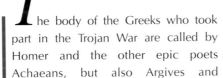

This venerable old man is, the inscription tells us, Nestor, the wise King of Pylos. (Detail). (Red-figure amphora, c. 480 BC).

Achilles surpassed the other Achaean leaders in good looks and manliness. His heroic figure, with its proud head and robust body, is here shown with something of the divine about it. (Red-figure amphora, c. 450 BC).

The weapons of Achilles

Peleus had given his son the helmet, the breastplate and the shield which the gods had given him when he married Thetis. He also gave him a spear of ash, a gift from Chiron, which was so heavy that none of the other Achaeans had the strength to lift it. Achilles also took with him the immortal horses of his father, Xanthus and Balius, who were the children of the Harpy Podarge and Zephyrus, and so were as swift as the wind.

intelligence and diplomacy. During the war, every time that the Achaeans had to solve some military or political problem, to take a difficult decision or to resort to trickery, Odysseus came into his own.

An important part in the war was played by two heroes called Ajax. The first, Ajax of Salamis, son of Telamon - brother of Peleus - always has the epithets 'great' or 'huge' attached to him. His shield, a veritable tower, could not be lifted by any other hero. His bastard brother was the first-class bowman Teucer, son of Telamon and Hesione, daughter of Laomedon. The second Ajax was surnamed Locrus and was believed to be the son of Oileus, from eastern Locris. Though they were not related, the two Ajaxes always fought side by side. The title of the most handsome and the most courageous of the Greeks belonged undoubtedly to Achilles. He was accompanied to Troy by his bosom friend Patroclus, son of Menoetius, and his beloved tutor Phoenix, son of Amyntor, king of the region of Thessaly which was known as 'Hellas'.

Many other heroes hastened to strengthen the army of the Achaeans with their ships and men. Among them were the fearless Diomedes, son of Tydeus, Idomeneus, son of Deucalion and grandson of Minos, Podalirius and Machaon, sons of Asclepius, Eumelus, son of Admetus, Polypoetes, son of Perithous, Tlepolemus, son of Heracles, Acamas and Demophon, sons of Theseus and Phaedra.

The wily Odysseus is shown deep in thought, with his petasos (hat) thrown back from his head and his sword in his sturdy hand. (Detail). (Red-figure pelike, c. 440 BC).

The **Trojans**

*I*n the Iliad, the adversaries of the Achaeans are called Trojans and Dardanians. By the first name, Homer seems to mean the inhabitants of Ilium, the capital of Troy, while by the second, the rest of the population of the country, though the distinction is not watertight. The King of Troy was the noble and lordly Priam, one of the sons of Laomedon. Priam was married to Hecuba, the daughter of Dymas, prince of Phrygia, who had borne him nineteen sons, among them Troilus, who fell at the hand of Achilles at the beginning of the war, the courageous Deiphobus, and Helenus. He had another 32 sons by other women, together with twelve daughters.

Hector, the eldest son of Priam, was the personification of the heroic warrior. His enemies feared him and his friends honoured him, because he protected the city with his bravery. By his beloved wife, Andromache, daughter of the king Eetion, he had a son, Astyanax.

As to Paris, the myth narrates that when Hecuba was pregnant with him, she dreamt that she gave birth to a burning torch which dripped blood and set fire to Troy. Aesacus, a bastard son of Priam who knew how to interpret dreams, advised his father to kill the child as soon as it was born, otherwise the days of Troy were numbered. The murder of the child was undertaken by a slave, who, however, took pity on him and left him on the slopes of Mt Ida. There he was fed by a she-bear and then was found by a

Hector prepares for battle. His mother, Hecuba, holds his helmet and spear for him, while his father, Priam, gives him his last words of advice. (Red-figure amphora, 510 - 500 BC).

Cassandra, the beautiful daughter of Priam, is one of the most tragic figures in Greek mythology. Here she embraces the statue of Athena, seeking protection from Ajax the Locrian, who is attempting to draw her to him by force. He is about to ravish her in the temple itself.
(Red-figure amphora, c. 450 BC).

In this fine vase-painting, Hermes presides over the removal from the field of battle of the dead Sarpedon, son of Zeus and Europa and wealthy King of Lycia. He is lifted by Hypnos (Sleep) and Thanatos (Death), the twin sons of Night. The dead Sarpedon, still a fine warrior, is shown as immense, his eyes unseeing and his teeth clenched, his limbs in the rigidity of death. Two hoplites, Leodamas and Hippolytus, attend as a guard of honour. (Red-figure krater, c. 510 BC).

shepherd, who brought him up. Later, Paris was recognised by his family and was received with great rejoicing at the palace. In the Iliad, Priam's second son is represented as handsome and charming to women, but also cowardly and quarrelsome.

Outstanding among the other Trojan heroes were Aeneas, son of Anchises and of the goddess Aphrodite, the aged, just Antenor, nephew of Priam, and his sons, particularly Agenor and Acamas, and Panthous, an elder of Troy, and his sons Hyperenor, Euphorbus, and Polydamas, a seer, the friend and counsellor of Hector.

Many allies of Troy, who arrived with their armies from distant lands, also took part in the terrible war. One of the most important of these was Sarpedon, the wealthy King of Lycia. Of Sarpedon it was said by some that he was the son of Zeus and Europa and brother of Minos and Rhadamanthus, by others that he was the son of Zeus and Laodamia, daughter of Bellerophon, by others that the son of Laodamia was the grandson of the first Sarpedon, and by yet others that there was only one Sarpedon, but that Zeus had granted him the privilege of living for three human generations. A faithful companion of Sarpedon was Glaucus, also a grandson of Bellerophon.

Cassandra

Cassandra, the beautiful daughter of Priam, was loved by Apollo, and agreed to be his on condition that he would give her the gift of prophecy. When, however, the god granted her wish, Cassandra refused to respond to his courtship. This angered Apollo, and, because he could not take back his gift, he laid a curse on her that no one would believe her prophecies, however true they might be. According to another myth, Cassandra was the twin of Helenus. One day, after some celebration, the parents left the children behind in the temple of Thymbraean Apollo. There, in the dark, snakes came and licked their ears, thus giving them the power to hear secret voices. Thus both brother and sister were endowed with the gift of prophecy.

The beginning of the **Campaign**

*After the tra-*ditional sacrifices,

Iphigenia approaches the altar, while behind her the deer has already appeared. In this scene, the sacrifice is to be performed by Agamemnon himself, as indicated by the sceptre which he holds. At the sacrifice, which is watched from on high by Apollo and Artemis, a young attendant assists. (Apulian krater, 370 - 350 BC).

the Achaeans set out for the land of Troy, but, since they did not know where exactly it was, they landed in Mysia and began to plunder it. At that time, the King of Mysia was Telephus, son of Heracles, who attacked them with his army and soon put them to flight, thus foiling their first expedition. During the course of the battle, however, Telephus was wounded in the thigh by the spear of Achilles and the wound refused to heal. Thus, having received an oracle that the wound could be healed only by the one who had inflicted it, he disguised himself as a beggar and went to Argos, where the kings were holding a meeting. Although to start with the Achaeans suspected that he was a Trojan spy, they finally agreed to help him. Then Odysseus, realising that the oracle did not mean Achilles himself, but his spear, scraped a little rust from the weapon on to the thigh of Telephus, and the wound closed. He, in order to show his thanks to the Achaeans for their good deed, showed them the way to Troy.

Eight years later, when the Achaeans had managed to gather once again at Aulis, Agamemnon entered, without realising it, a grove sacred to Artemis and killed a sacred deer. He boasted, moreover, that not even the goddess herself would have aimed so well. Artemis in her fury sent a great calm, so that the ships of the Achaeans were unable to spread their sails. Then the seer Calchas revealed to them that in order to placate her, Iphigenia, the most beautiful of the daughters of Agamemnon would have to be sacrificed on her altar. After much hesitation, Agamemnon sent a message to Clytemnestra telling her to bring their daughter to Aulis, allegedly because Achilles wished to marry her. Delighted, the queen soon reached the camp, together with Iphigenia, where she discovered that Achilles had no intention of marrying the girl. An-

When Telephus was accused of being a spy of the Trojans, he snatched up Orestes, the son of Agamemnon, and took up his position as a suppliant at the altar of Zeus, threatening to kill him if Achilles did not cure him and the Achaeans did not allow him to return home. Here the hero, with a bandage to indicate the place of his wound, sits at the altar. The young Orestes, in his arms, stretches out his hands towards Agamemnon, who is arriving on the scene from the left. (Red-figure pelike, c. 450 BC).

Protesilaus, the first Achaean to lose his life on Trojan soil, as he jumps from the prow of the ship on to dry land. (Silver coin of Thebes in Phthiotis, 302 - 286 BC).

gered that he had been used as bait, the hero promised Clytemnestra that he would not permit the sacrifice to happen, but the army disagreed. It was Iphigenia herself who finally found the solution. Seeing so many men ready to lose their lives at Troy, she went to the altar of sacrifice of her own free will. But at the moment Calchas raised the knife, Artemis snatched the girl away and put a most beautiful deer in her place. Iphigenia she took to the country of the Taurians, where she made her a priestess in her temple.

The Achaeans, now with a fair wind, reached the Troad. But, since there was an oracle to the effect that whoever was first to set foot on Trojan soil would immediately meet his death, no one took the first step. Then Odysseus jumped down from the ship, having first thrown a shield on to the ground to stand on. Fooled by this device, the Thessalian Protesilaus, who was to slay many Trojans, then jumped down, but as he had been in fact the first to touch the soil of Troy, he was soon himself slain by the spear of Hector. The Achaeans then attempted to settle their differences with the Trojans peacefully, but without success. And so the war began.

Protesilaus

Protesilaus, son of Iphiclus and King of Phylace, left for Troy on the day after his marriage to Laodamia, the daughter of Acastus, who, when she learnt of the death of her husband, refused to believe it. Protesilaus too was tormented in the Underworld by his love of Laodamia, so he asked Pluto to allow him to spend three hours with her. The god agreed and, after the three hours were over, Protesilaus asked his beloved to go with him to Hades. She, without hesitation, took his sword and committed suicide.

The wrath of **Achilles**

Achilles, in spite of his anger, agreed to hand over his slave-girl Briseis to Agamemnon, after Athena has intervened. Here the son of Peleus and Thetis, seated and tightly wrapped in his cloak, watches the two heralds who are taking the slave-girl from his tent. In front of him stands some unnamed hero. (Red-figure kylix, c. 480 BC).

For nine years the Achaeans besieged the walls of Troy without making any progress. In the tenth year, Chryses, priest of Apollo, presented himself at the Achaean camp, bearing with him large amounts of valuables in order to exchange these for his daughter, Chryseis, who had been taken prisoner in some raid of the Achaeans on Thebes, a city of the Troad, and had been given as a slave to Agamemnon. Everyone, the kings and the ordinary soldiers alike, showed themselves willing to return his daughter to the old man, with the exception of Agamemnon, who brutally drove out the aged priest. Then Apollo, in order to punish the Achaeans, began to kill men and animals with his bow. Nine days later, Calchas declared that in order to placate the god, they must let Chryseis go free, without any ransom. Agamemnon was forced to give in, but demanded to take in her place the slave-girl of Achilles, Briseis. The two kings exchanged harsh words over this, until Achilles said that he would hand over Briseis but, because of the insult, he would withdraw from the battle.

Without the intrepid Achilles, the Achaeans were vulnerable. And so Zeus, who wanted the Trojans to win, sent a dream to tell Agamemnon that the time had come for him to take the city. Thus the two armies prepared themselves for battle. First, Paris boasted that he would meet in combat any of the Achaeans; Menelaus accepted the challenge. It was agreed that the war should stop, and that whichever of the two men was the victor would win Helen. The agreement was sealed with oaths and the duel began. But when the moment came when Menelaus was dragging Paris by the helmet towards the Achaean camp, his protectress intervened, snatched him up, and bore him back to the palace. At the same time, in order to ensure that the war would not stop, Athena,

144

Chryseis, the beautiful slave-girl of Agamemnon, followed by her father, the priest Chryses. (Red-figure skyphos, c. 480 BC).

The gods and the Trojan War

The gods of Olympus had in the matter of the Trojan War, as in everything else, their own personal likes and dislikes. Hera and Athena were on the side of the Achaeans, since Paris had insulted them by giving the apple to Aphrodite. Of the other gods, Poseidon, Hermes, and Hephaestus supported the Achaeans, while Apollo, Artemis, Ares, and Aphrodite gave all the help they could to the Trojans.

taking the form of a Trojan, persuaded the Lycian Pandarus to fire an arrow at Menelaus, in spite of the fact that the truce still held. The hero's wound was not serious, but this breach of the truce extinguished every hope of peace. In the battle which followed, Hector measured his strength against Ajax the son of Telamon, without either emerging victorious.

On the next day, when the conflict began, Zeus strictly forbade any of the gods to help their protegés. Then he travelled in his chariot to Ida, the mountain above Troy, where he sat down to watch the contest. Until midday, the battle was evenly balanced, but later Zeus began to give new heart to Hector and the Trojans. And when he saw Hera and Athena, who had descended to the earth to support the Achaeans, he threatened to burn them up with his thunderbolts.

As soon as darkness fell, the council of the Achaeans sent a delegation to Achilles, offering him absolute satisfaction on behalf of Agamemnon, but the hero refused to be reconciled to the commander-in-chief. The same night, Odysseus and Diomedes slipped into the enemy camp and killed Rhesus, King of the Thracians, who had arrived at Troy the previous day with his army. Later, they stole his pure white horses, which shone like sunbeams, ran like the wind, and could become invisible.

Menelaus attacks Paris with bared sword. Paris runs away, looking behind him. The Trojan warrior is supported by two goddesses, Artemis on the right and Aphrodite on the left. (Red-figure kylix, c. 485 BC).

The death of **Patroclus**

*T*he next morning, the foremost champions of the

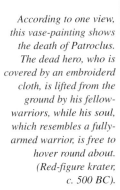

According to one view, this vase-painting shows the death of Patroclus. The dead hero, who is covered by an embroiderd cloth, is lifted from the ground by his fellow-warriors, while his soul, which resembles a fully-armed warrior, is free to hover round about. (Red-figure krater, c. 500 BC).

Achaeans, Agamemnon, Odysseus, and Diomedes, were wounded on the field of battle, while the Trojans began to come dangerously close to the ships of their enemies. In the meantime, Zeus, believing that none of the gods would dare to disobey him and intervene in the war, turned his attention to distant countries. So Poseidon took the opportunity to embolden the Achaeans, who stemmed the onslaught of the Trojans.

Hera, who could not bear to see Zeus give the victory to the Trojans, also decided to intervene. Having bathed, she perfumed herself, put on the breast-band of Aphrodite, which aroused erotic passion, and presented herself before him, supposedly to seek his permission to visit Oceanus and Tethys. Delighted, the god asked her to lie with him, and she, after some pretended hesitation, agreed. Later, when Zeus was sleeping in the embrace of his wife, Hypnos ('Sleep'), on Hera's instructions, hastened to inform Poseidon that he could, unhindered, continue to give heart to the Achaeans. Thus, Ajax succeeded in hurling a huge rock at Hector and laying him out on the ground, so that the Trojans had to drag him, with great difficulty, as far as the banks of the Scamander in order to rescue him.

When the king of the gods awoke and cast a glance at the plain of Troy, he realised at once what had happened. Although Hera managed to persuade him that she was not responsible for the acts of his brother, Zeus sent her back to Olympus and warned Poseidon to take himself away from Troy. He then gave orders to Apollo to put Hector back

A little before the two friends part for ever, Patroclus, wearing his companion's armour and standing before the altar, turns towards the seated Achilles, who is offering a libation. (Red-figure stamnos, early 5th century BC).

As soon as Zeus stopped supervising the battles between the Greeks and Trojans, Poseidon hastened to Ilium in order to embolden his favourites. Here we see the god between the two Ajaxes gesturing spiritedly as he addresses Ajax, son of Telamon, behind whom stands his brother, the archer Teucer. (Black-figure kylix, c. 540 BC).

Hera presents herself to Zeus adorned and perfumed, in order to kindle his desire and to force him to turn his gaze away from the Trojan plain. He, without suspecting her cunning plan, welcomes her. (Metope from Temple E at Selinunte, c. 460 BC).

The new panoply of Achilles

After the theft of the arms of Achilles by Hector, Thetis ordered new weapons from Hephaestus for her son. The god shut himself in his workshop and forged for the hero a breastplate, a helmet, greaves, and a shield, on which he depicted land and sea, the sun, the moon, the starry heavens, fields and palaces, and all round the rim, the boundless Ocean.

on his feet. With the god leading them, Hector and the Trojans then made an onslaught on the ships of the Achaeans.

At this critical moment, Patroclus, urged on by Nestor, asked Achilles to give him his weapons and to allow him to fight with the Myrmidons. Achilles agreed, but asked him to stop the contest as soon as he had driven off the enemy.

The sight of Patroclus with this weaponry struck terror into the Trojans, who, believing Achilles had re-entered the battle, began to give ground. At once, Patroclus charged against the Lycians, duelled with Sarpedon, and killed him. Then, forgetting what his friend had told him, he continued the attack. He almost succeeded in setting foot in the citadel of Troy, but Apollo intervened by striking him hard on the back and beginning to throw far from him his armour and weapons, one by one. The hero was still dazed by the blow of the god when Euphorbus, son of Panthous, took aim at him with his spear, while he was actually killed by Hector. As soon as Patroclus fell dead to the earth, Hector buckled on the armour of Achilles. At the same time, a fierce battle broke out over which side would take the hero's body. In spite of the efforts of the Achaeans, the dead Patroclus was in danger of falling into the hands of the Trojans. But Achilles, learning of the death of his friend, uttered a cry of such ferocity that the Trojans took to their heels in terror. Thus the Achaeans took the lifeless corpse to the tent of Achilles, who mourned inconsolably.

147

Achilles binds up a wound for his beloved friend Patroclus. (Attic red-figure kylix - interior - signed by the potter Sosias and attributed to the Sosias Painter, c.500 BC).

Achilles kills Penthesilea, Queen of the Amazons.
(Attic red-figure kylix - interior - attributed to the Penthesilea Painter, c.455 BC).

Hector and Achilles

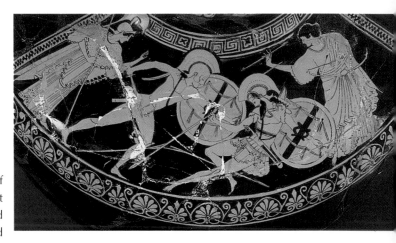

With a violence generated by his grief at the death of his friend, Achilles attacks Hector, who has almost collapsed, with his naked sword. The mortal combat is watched by Athena, on the left, and Apollo, on the right. (Red-figure hydria, c. 490 BC).

*I*n spite of the fact that Thetis had warned Achilles that Fate had ordained that he would lose his life if he killed Hector, the hero was determined to avenge the death of Patroclus. Thus, when he had lamented all night long the loss of his companion, he went at dawn to the council of the Achaeans and told Agamemnon that he was ready to fight again at his side. The same morning, Zeus announced to the rest of the gods that his command that they should keep out of the war no longer applied.

In the meantime, Achilles, with the arms which his mother had given him, set upon the Trojans and began to slaughter them without pity. And the gods, who had arrived at the plain of Troy, started to fight among themselves. In the end the victors were those gods who protected the Achaeans. The Trojans, pursued, took refuge in their city. Agenor alone attempted to withstand the uncontrollable Achilles, but Apollo snatched him out of harm's way. Then the god, taking on the form of Agenor, lured Achilles far from the gates, so that the rest of the Trojans could huddle inside the fortress.

Now not a single Trojan remained outside the walls - apart from Hector. In vain did his parents implore him to spare his own life, and them. The hero was going to face, all alone, his fearful opponent. But when Achilles, who had chased after Apollo in vain, returned and rushed upon him, Hector took to flight. Three times he ran round the circuit of the fortress, without Achilles being able to catch him. But the hour of the Trojan's death had come. Athena, with the leave of her father, took on the form of Deiphobus and coming up to Hector, told him that he had come outside the walls to help him.

Achilles, lying on an elaborately decorated couch and turning towards the young charioteer on his left, does not seem to have realised yet that Priam has come to beg to be given the body of his son. The dead Hector lies abandoned in the dust. *(Red-figure skyphos, c. 485 - 480 BC).*

Although Achilles has buried his spear in her neck, the brave Queen of the Amazons, Penthesilea, still has the strength to direct her own spear against him. The eyes of the hero, which are fixed on hers, are a reminder of the ancient tradition of the love which was engendered in his heart when he gazed on the radiant beauty of the dead woman. (Black-figure amphora, c. 530 - 525 BC).

Blending together events belonging to different times and places, the vase-painter here shows us Achilles running to mount his chariot, next to the charioteer, to the back of which the body of Hector has been tied. On the left, Priam and Hecuba mourn, while in the middle Iris comes flying to bring the message of the gods. On the right we see the tomb of Patroclus and his winged soul. (Black-figure hydria, c. 510 BC).

Fooled by this, he came to a halt, to measure up to the Achaean. In a short time, Achilles had taken his revenge. His spear wounded Hector mortally in the neck.

Achilles' treatment of the dead Hector was particularly harsh. He stripped him, tied him behind his chariot, and dragged him as far as the Achaean camp, where he threw him on to the earth. He then burnt the body of Patroclus and held funeral games in his honour.

When twelve days had passed, Zeus sent a message by Thetis to Achilles that the gods were outraged by his behaviour and advising him to surrender the body of Hector to the Trojans. The hero raised no objection to this and, when Priam, informed by Iris, arrived at his tent, he received him with respect and kindness. When they had eaten, drunk and slept, Achilles promised that the war would stop for as many days as were required for the funeral. The king left the camp of the Achaeans, bearing the body of his son.

Penthesilea

Immediately after the funeral of Hector, the Queen of the Amazons, Penthesilea, daughter of Ares, arrived at Troy to support Priam. Fearlessly the Amazon attacked the Achaeans, not stopping even when she found herself face to face with the unvanquished Achilles. Achilles killed Penthesilea after a hard contest, but when he looked upon her beautiful face, he was filled with sorrow, because it occurred to him that she could have been a worthy partner for him. So, instead of taking her weapons and casting her to the dogs and birds of prey, as was customary in war, he gave her body to the Trojans to bury with appropriate honours.

The end of **Achilles**

Ajax, son of Telamon, the hero who was distinguished by his physical and mental powers, lifts on to his shoulders the huge body of the dead Achilles in order to take him to the Myrmidons. (From the handle of the François krater, c. 570 BC).

*T*he Trojans took new courage when another ally, the brave and handsome Memnon, King of Ethiopia, son of Eos and Tithonus - brother of Priam - appeared on the scene. But their optimism was not destined to last long. When Memnon killed Antilochus, the beloved friend of Achilles, he was furiously attacked by the Achaean hero. While they duelled, Thetis and Eos ascended Olympus and each pleaded with Zeus to save their son. But Fate had already made up her mind. The one who would lose his life was Memnon. All his mother could do now was to ask Zeus to grant him the gift of immortality, to which the god agreed.

The death of the Ethiopian king was destined to be followed by that of Achilles. As the Trojans turned to flight in terror, Achilles rushed forward to enter the fortress, but before the gates Apollo was waiting for him. Having ordered Paris to aim at the hero, he directed the arrow so that it pierced Achilles in a fatal spot. And so the son of Thetis, the bravest of the Achaeans, fell lifeless to the ground.

At once a fierce battle broke out around his corpse. In the end, Ajax managed to lift the body on to his shoulders and to run to the Achaean camp, covered by Odysseus. There the Achaeans washed off the blood, while Thetis and her sisters the Nereids and the Muses mourned him in so heartbreaking a fashion that no one was able to hold back his tears. For seventeen whole days and nights mortals and goddesses wept for Achilles; on the eighteenth they put his body on the funeral pyre. As soon as the flames had died down, they collected his bones, washed them in wine and placed them together with the bones of Patroclus in a gold amphora which had been

Amid a huge tumult, tradition says, Thetis and her sisters the Nereids rose from the sea to mourn for Achilles. In this picture, the goddesses, round the bed of the dead hero, tear their hair, while the lyre which one of them holds is the accompaniment to their sorrowful song.
(Corinthian hydria, c. 570 BC).

Bending, Ajax, with a thoughtful and sorrowful air, fixes the handle of his sword in the earth. In the desolation of the landscape, a palm tree and the hero's armour, which looks as though it is being worn by an invisible warrior, stand as the sole witnesses to his act.
(Black-figure amphora, c. 530 BC).

made by Hephaestus. Then they raised a huge burial mound at Sigeum, a spit of land on the Hellespont, and held funeral games in his honour.

After the games, Thetis decided to present the armour of her son to the worthiest of the Achaeans. Of all of them, only two dared to claim it: Ajax and Odysseus. Since, however, neither would accept the superiority of the other, the wise Nestor proposed that the Trojans should give a decision, since they would not be influenced by personal likes or antipathies. What happened was that while some Achaeans were spying below the walls of Troy, they heard two Trojan women commenting on the latest feat of Ajax and Odysseus - the taking of the body of Achilles out of enemy hands. The two women agreed that the one who had shown the greater courage was Odysseus, and so the panoply was given to the King of Ithaca. The slight to Ajax was, of course, a great one, and as soon as darkness fell, he set out to kill the Achaean kings.

Eos, the winged goddess of the dawn, sadly lifts the corpse of her beloved son, Memnon.
(Interior of a red-figure kylix, c. 485 BC).

At the last moment, however, Athena confused his mind and all he succeeded in doing was to kill the sheep and cattle of the Achaeans. At dawn, when he came to his senses, he realised that all his fellow-warriors would laugh at him for his deed and that his reputation had been destroyed. So the great Ajax fixed his sword in the ground and, falling on it, killed himself.

Tithonus

When Eos, the goddess of the dawn, fell in love with Tithonus, she asked Zeus to make him immortal, but she forgot to ask at the same time for the gift of eternal youth. As the years passed, the hair of Tithonus turned white, and though Eos continued to care for him, she no longer went to his bed. When he reached extreme old age, she changed him into a cicada, so that she could at least take pleasure in his voice.

Philoctetes and Neoptolemus at Troy

In a desolate landscape on Lemnos, Philoctetes sits, melancholy, on a rock, with the bow and quiver of Heracles resting beside him. With his left hand he is raising his injured foot. (Red-figure lekythos, 430 - 420 BC).

*O*ne day, Calchas, the seer of the Achaeans, revealed to Odysseus that Helenus, son of Priam, was the only one who knew the oracles about the fall of Troy. So Odysseus laid an ambush for Helenus, took him prisoner and, threatening him with death, forced him to reveal the secret: Ilium would fall only if the Achaeans had in their possession the weapons and arrows of Heracles. These weapons belonged to Philoctetes, son of Poeas, from Magnesia in Thessaly, who had set out for Troy with his seven ships together with the Achaean fleet. But, as they were heading towards Troy, the Achaeans put in at an island called Chryse, in order to offer sacrifice to the goddess of the same name. There a snake bit the foot of Philoctetes, and his companions, unable to stand his cries of anguish or the stench of the wound, abandoned him all alone on Lemnos. For nine years the leaders of the Achaeans had thought nothing about his fate, but now they had to find him and take the weapons of Heracles. So they sent Odysseus and Diomedes to Lemnos, where they took the arms by stealth. Philoctetes, not wishing to remain in this wild place without his bow, with which he killed birds and animals in order to live, followed them to Troy. As soon as he arrived at the Achaean camp, Philoctetes was cured by Machaon, entered the battle, and, having slain many Trojans, killed Paris in single combat. According to the prophecies of Helenus, there was one more condition for the Achaeans to take Troy: that Neoptolemus, the son of Achilles and Deidamia, who

Odysseus delivers to Neoptolemus, the son of Achilles, the panoply of his father. The young man examines them carefully and with obvious satisfaction.
(Interior of a red-figure kylix, c. 490 BC).

Detail from the scene of the theft of the two Palladiums - the original and a copy of it - by Odysseus and Diomedes.
(Red-figure amphora, 490 - 480 BC).

The goddess Athena casts a last searching glance at the Trojan Horse, which is shown only up to the chest. Its construction, on the advice of the goddess, was decisive for the outcome of the Trojan War. (Interior of a red-figure kylix, 470 - 460 BC).

live on Skyros with his mother and grandfather, should fight below its walls. The mission of travelling to Skyros was again undertaken by Odysseus. He succeeded without great difficulty in returning with Neoptolemus to Troy. In spite of his youth, Neoptolemus distinguished himself at once for his prudence and, of course, for his courage in battle. Wearing the armour of his father, which Odysseus had given him, he sowed terror and death among his enemies.

Also decisive for the outcome of the war was the intervention of Athena, who counselled Odysseus that the Achaeans should construct a large wooden horse, the famous Trojan Horse. Within a few days, Epeius, son of Panopeus from Phocis, had set up a huge horse, with secret doors on either side, in which thousands of warriors could hide, bearing the carved inscription 'Thankoffering of the Greeks to Athena'. The best of the warriors then hid inside it, while the rest of the Achaeans set fire to their tents, embarked on their ships and, in the night, set out into the open sea, to give the impression that they were returning to Greece. In fact they hid at Tenedos, on a beach invisible from Troy.

The Palladium

A third oracle of Helenus said that Troy would be safe as long as the Palladium, the wooden statue kept in the temple of Pallas Athena, was inside the citadel. The Palladium was stolen one night by Odysseus and Diomedes. Troy was now at the mercy of the Achaeans. The idea that some ancient statue of a god protects a city is a natural one and is to be found among many peoples. The statue is the being of the deity, and so its departure from the city means that it is also being abandoned by the god.

The fall of Troy

A scene from the tragic hours of the fall of Troy. In the centre, Priam, sitting at an altar, wounded, puts his hands to his head in despair, while his grandson Astyanax lies, already dead, on his knees. In front of him, Neoptolemus, drawing him by the shoulder, prepares to put him to death with his sword, which he raises menacingly. In front of the altar, one of the sons of Priam lies dead. On the left, Cassandra and the other Trojan women, kneeling before the statue of Athena, plead to be spared. On the right, a Trojan woman prepares to strike one of the Greeks with a piece of wood. (Red-figure kalpe, 480 - 475 BC).

The next morning, the Trojans could not believe their eyes. The Achaeans' camp was deserted. Hesitantly at first, and then more boldly, they opened the gates and began to go down to the plain, where their astonished eyes fell upon the enormous horse. At that moment some shepherds found Sinon, cousin of Odysseus, who had stayed behind to lead the Trojans astray, on the seashore. When questioned, Sinon, who had been well coached by the wily King of Ithaca, provide the appropriate answers, so that in the end he persuaded them to put the horse inside the city. Without loss of time, the Trojans demolished part of the walls to make room for the horse to enter, and, with much toil, pulled it as far as the palace of Priam. At that moment Cassandra raced up to them, shouting that there were Achaeans hidden inside the horse, but no one paid any attention to her words. In vain did Laocoon, a seer and the priest of Apollo and brother of Anchises, hurl a spear into the belly of the horse and try to warn the Trojans of the impending disaster. Later, while Laocoon was offering sacrifice to Poseidon by the seashore, two huge serpents emerged from the waves and devoured him and one of his sons. Now convinced that they were safe, the Trojans, who believed that the priest had been punished for striking with his spear the horse which was dedicated to Athena, gave themselves up to merrymaking which lasted all day long.

At midnight, Sinon went up on to the funeral mound of Achilles and held high a burning torch. This was the signal which the Achaean fleet, hidden at Tenedos, had been waiting for to return to the shores of Troy. At the same time, Odysseus, Neop-

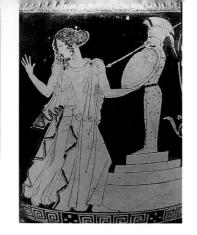

In vain did Laocoon, seer and priest of Apollo, attempt to warn the Trojans of the disaster they would suffer at the hands of the Achaeans hidden in the Trojan Horse. Later, at the feast held by the Trojans in the belief that they were now safe, two huge snakes appeared, wound themselves round Laocoon and tore apart him and one of his children. The elder son is making his escape on the right. (Laocoon group, 1st century AD).

Aeneas

One of the few Trojans to survive the fall of the city was Aeneas, the son of Anchises and Aphrodite. It is said that when the hero fell into the hands of the Achaeans, they were unwilling to harm him because they knew how much Zeus loved him. So they allowed him to go, taking with him whatever was most valuable that he had hidden at home. He took on his back his paralysed father and left the city, followed by his wife, Creousa, and his children. After many wanderings, Aeneas reached Italy, where he, or a descendant of his, founded Rome.

tolemus, Diomedes, Menelaus, Philoctetes and the other heroes who had been hiding in the horse opened the secret doors, jumped down to the ground, and hastened to open the gates of Troy so that their army could enter. With lightning speed the Achaeans poured into the houses, broke down doors, and began the slaughter. Innumerable Trojans lost their life that

Two of the scenes in relief which adorn the body of an amphora, in which we are shown concisely, but disturbingly, the tragic fate of the women and infants of Troy after its fall. The Achaeans, fully-armed, rush upon them with incredible ferocity, piercing the childrens' bodies with the sword and slaughtering the mothers or carrying them off into slavery in distant lands. (Amphora with scenes in relief, c. 670 BC).

night. Neoptolemus killed Priam and snatched up Astyanax, the son of Hector, from the arms of his mother, Andromache, and threw him from the walls of the city. Cassandra also met with a tragic fate. The beautiful prophetess, who had taken refuge in the temple of Athena, was seized by the hair by Locrian Ajax and ravished in the precinct of the temple. Menelaus and Odysseus set out to find Helen at the house of Deiphobus, who had married her after the death of Paris. According to one version of the myth, as soon as Menelaus came face to face with his wife, whose infidelity had been the cause of the death of so many brave warriors, he drew his sword to kill her. But Helen, without fear, bared her breast, and Menelaus, succumbing to her beauty, was reconciled to her and took her with him to his ship.

The return of the heroes

After wars and wanderings in distant lands, Menelaus returns to his own country with Helen. (Black-figure amphora, c. 540 BC).

*A*fter they had burned the city, the Achaeans shared out among themselves the valuable spoil and took the women of Troy as slaves. Thus, Andromache was given to Neoptolemus, Cassandra to Agamemnon and so on. Then the heroes prepared to return to their homelands. But Athena, who had supported them for so many years, was now angry with them because of the looting of the sanctuaries of Troy and was plotting their destruction. The first bad sign was a quarrel which broke out between Menelaus and Agamemnon. Since the two brothers were unable to reach agreement, the army was divided into two. Some of the Achaeans in their ships followed Menelaus, who left at once, while others stayed on at Troy together with Agamemnon.

Agamemnon and his companions, having offered sacrifice to Athena without succeeding in placating her, spread their sails, in spite of the bad omens. Initially, the weather seemed good, but off Caphereus on Euboea a terrible tempest blew up and many ships were sunk. Locrian Ajax, whose ship had been sunk by a thunderbolt of Athena, found himself struggling with the waves, but Poseidon took pity on him and helped him to climb on to a rock and escape. But because the hero boasted that he had been saved in defiance of Athena, who was seeking to destroy him, Poseidon was angered, and, taking up his trident, split in two the rock on which the hero was standing. Thus the arrogant Ajax lost his life.

The two kings who had left Troy together with Menelaus, Nestor and Diomedes, reached home in a few days. Menelaus, however, wandered with Helen for eight

Without mercy, Queen Clytemnestra raises the axe to kill Cassandra, the beautiful daughter of Priam, whom Agamemnon has brought with him from Troy to Argos as his mistress. (Interior of a red-figure kylix, c. 430 BC).

Cassandra, chased by Locrian Ajax, seeks sanctuary at the statue of Athena - but in vain, because Ajax seizes her by the hair and drags her down, in order to ravish her in the temple. For this sacrilegious act, the Locrians would pay a heavy tribute for a thousand years. (Apulian krater, c. 350 BC).

whole years before being permitted to see Sparta again. But there is another version of the story according to which Helen never set foot in Troy. The woman whom Paris abducted was no more than a likeness of her, made by Hera out of cloud, because she wanted to take vengeance on him for his preference for Aphrodite. The real Helen was taken by Hermes to Proteus, King of Egypt, to keep her safe until the time came for her to return, untouched, to her husband. After the death of Proteus, however, his son Theoclymenus wanted to make Helen his own by force. At this critical moment Menelaus, who was still wandering the seas, even though seven years had passed since the fall of Troy, arrived in Egypt. There he found Helen, and, learning of what had happened, rescued her from the hands of the king and returned together with her to Sparta.

Of the rest of the Achaeans, Neoptolemus and Idomeneus did not encounter any great difficulties in their journey home, while Philoctetes was wrecked on the rocks of southern Italy, where he settled permanently.

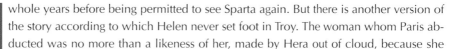

The tribute of the Locrians

Three years after the return of the Locrian army from the Troad, a terrible famine fell upon the land. The Delphic oracle revealed to the Locrians that Athena was angry because of the rape of Cassandra by Ajax in her temple, and that to placate her they must send each year, for a thousand years, two virgins to serve in the temple of the goddess at Troy. During the Phocian War (345 BC), the Locrians decided that a thousand years had passed, and stopped sending the girls. A century later, however, a new disaster overtook them. The earth swould not yield its fruit and crippled or monstrous children started to be born. Since they then received an oracle to the effect that Athena had not yet been satisfied, the Locrians continued to send their daughters to Troy until around 150 BC.

159

The murder of **Agamemnon** and the revenge of **Orestes**

In his palace, trapped in a piece of cloth without openings, Agamemnon has already sustained the first blow from Aegisthus, who has seized him by the hair and is preparing to give him the final blow. Behind Agamemnon, Electra (?) gestures in despair. (Red-figure krater, 470 - 460 BC).

*T*he ships of Agamemnon were among the few which, with the help of Hera, were spared from the storm at Caphereus. But the leader of the Achaeans was destined to lose his life in his own palace. As long as the war lasted, his wife, Clytemnestra, was conducting a love affair with Aegisthus, son of Thyestes. So as soon as they heard that the commander-in-chief of the Achaeans was returning from Troy, they resolved to get rid of him. Thus, the unsuspecting Agamemnon was murdered by Aegisthus, or, as some say, by the hand of his wife.

Meanwhile, Orestes, the son of Agamemnon and Clytemnestra, was growing up in Phocis with King Strophius, where his mother had sent him so that he should not witness her misdoings. Eight years after the murder of Agamemnon, Orestes arrived at Argos together with his beloved friend Pylades, son of Strophius. There he was reunited with his sister Electra, and took vengeance for the death of his father by killing both Aegisthus and Clytemnestra. Then Orestes, pursued by the Erinyes (Furies), sombre and implacable goddesses of the Underworld who were seeking to punish him, fled to Athens, seeking the protection of Athena. The goddess convened a court at the Areopagus consisting of distinguished Athenians, with herself presiding, which acquitted the hero. The Erinyes, who had been greatly angered by this verdict, were placated by Athena and from then on were converted into benign goddesses, protectors of vegetation and fruitfulness with the name of 'Eumenides'.

However, in spite of the mediation of Athena, some of the Erinyes would not agree to settle in Attica as Eumenides and continued the pursuit of Orestes. The only hope, as Apollo revealed to him, was to steal the ancient wooden statue of Artemis from

Orestes buries his sword in the breast of Aegisthus, tearing him off the throne of Agamemnon, which he has for years usurped. Orestes' sister Chrysothemis flees in despair. (Red-figure pelike, c. 500 BC).

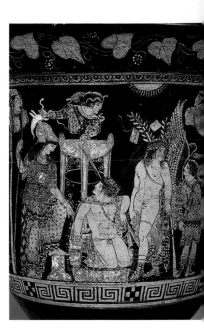

This scene shows the rite of the purification of Orestes in the sanctuary of Delphi. On the left of Orestes is Athena and on the right, Apollo and one of the Furies. Behind the Delphic tripod another Fury can be seen, while up above, Leto and Pylades are shown, with the sun half-hidden in between them. (Paestum krater, 350 - 340 BC).

This vase-painting depicts the meeting of Electra and Orestes at the tomb of Agamemnon. Electra sits in sadness on the steps of the monument, where she has left her gifts in honour of the dead. Orestes enters from the left, holding his spear and a phial. On the right, Hermes leans on his herald's wand and holds a wreath. (Lucanian pelike, c. 350 BC).

the sanctuary of the goddess in Scythia, in the country of the Taurians, and to bring it to Attica. Thus Orestes and his inseparable friend Pylades set out for the land of the Taurians. In that distant country, where it was the custom to sacrifice strangers, Orestes and Pylades were taken prisoner by some of the local people and were taken to the temple of Artemis. The priestess of the goddess was Iphigenia, the sister of Orestes, whose family thought she was dead. It was Iphigenia's duty to sacrifice the two young men, but she agreed to let one of them go free if he would travel to Argos to tell her brother to come and save her, because she could no longer bear to lead people to slaughter. Much moved, Orestes revealed to her his identity and then, at great risk, managed to leave with his sister and the wooden statue of Artemis, which he installed in a temple which he founded in honour of the goddess at Brauron in Attica. After all these escapades, Orestes was deemed fit to ascend the throne of his father and to rule until he was 70 - or 90 - years old, when he died from a snake bite.

Tisamenus

While Menelaus was still in the Troad, he had promised Neoptolemus that he would give him his only daughter, Hermione, as a wife, without knowing that Tyndareus had already married her to Orestes. Thus, when he returned from the war, he was forced to divorce his daughter from his nephew and give her to the son of Achilles. Later, however, Neoptolemus was killed at Delphi, and Hermione returned to Orestes and presented him with a son, whom his father named Tisamenus (from a verb meaning 'to take vengeance'), to remind him of the revenge which he had taken for the murder of Agamemnon.

161

THE ODYSSEY
The Odyssey
THE ODYSSEY

THE ODYSSEY

Odysseus, resting his foot on a rock, leans forward and gestures as if talking to someone. In his left hand he holds a scabbard and sword. (Seal-stone, 4th century BC).

*T*he Odyssey, the second epic creation of Homer, narrates the tribulations and feats of Odysseus from the time when he left Troy with his fleet until the moment when he set foot again on the soil of Ithaca. The poet must have drawn on earlier epic compositions - which, since they were not written down, were soon forgotten, so that today we can only guess at their existence - for the episodes in the journey. However, from the 7th century BC it was the Homeric epic which told the Greeks, and later the whole world, how Odysseus wandered for ten whole years before setting eyes on his homeland again. The mythical adventures of Odysseus start out from real places. From Troy, he went to Thrace, to the country of the Cicones, a people who lived between the Hebrus and the Nestus, and from there to Maleas. From that point on, Homer describes countries in the world of the imagination. However, in spite of the fact that the Odyssey is purely a work of the poet's imagination, the attempt to prove that it is the first written record of Greek geography had already begun in ancient times. In more modern times, scholars and amateur students of Homer have put forward innumerable theories, which would have Odysseus travelling to the four points of the compass, from the fjords of Norway to Africa, Canada, or the Gulf of Mexico. Indicative of the pointlessness of the attempt to pinpoint on the map the places which the hero visited is the saying of the great mathematician and geographer of the 3rd Century BC Eratosthenes: 'Only when you manage to discover who the craftsman was who sewed the bag which Aeolus used to imprison the winds for the benefit of Odysseus will you identify the places the hero visited'.

The meeting of Odysseus with his wife, Penelope. She, seated with one leg over the other, rests her head on her hand in hopelessness, since she has not yet recognised the hero who is standing before her in the form of a beggar. ('Melian' relief, c. 460 - 450 BC).

According to the myth, the family of Odysseus was descended from Cephalus, the handsome son of Deioneus, King of Phocis, or, according to another account, of Hermes and Creusa, daughter of Erechtheus. Cephalus took part in the expedition of Amphitryon, father of Heracles, to the islands of the Taphians, and the latter in order to reward him, gave him an island to settle on, which from then on took the name of Cephalonia. But since the hero had no children, he went to the oracle of Delphi, where the god commanded him to go back to his island and to have intercourse with the first female he came across. The first female he encountered was a she-bear, which, when he united himself with it, changed into a woman and, nine months later, brought into the world Arcesius. Arcesius's son was Laertes, who had a son by his wife, Anticlea - Odysseus. Odysseus's grandfather on his mother's side was the famous thief Autolycus, son of Hermes.

As a hero, Odysseus united courage with quickness of wit and readiness of tongue. He was, that is, the incarnation of the ideal of the period, which required that men should be distinguished by their deeds and their words. The epithets which usually accompany his name in the epic are 'renowned for the use of the spear', 'shrewd in battle', 'courageous'. However, since his subsequent history and tribulations were well known, he is already described in the Iliad as 'wily', 'enduring much', and 'persevering'. An epithet which is applied exclusively to Odysseus is *polyainos*, meaning 'much praised'.

For years on end, after the taking of Troy, Odysseus wandered over unknown seas, without ever abandoning his longing to return to Ithaca. Even when he was living with the beautiful Calypso, who had promised to make him immortal if he stayed with her, he would go down to the shore every morning, sit on the rocks and gaze out to sea, shedding bitter tears as he remembered his homeland. (Cheekpiece of a helmet, 425 - 400 BC).

163

Among the **Cicones**, the **Lotus-eaters**, and in the land of the **Cyclopes**

Polyphemus, vast and terrifying like an ogre in a fairytale, tries with one hand to pull out the branch which Odysseus has poked into his eye, while in the other he is still holding the cup of wine. (Early Attic krater, c. 670 BC).

When Odysseus had left Troy behind, his ships were driven by the winds to Ismarus in Thrace, a city of the Cicones, which he looted. He spared only the family of Maron, priest of Apollo, who, as a mark of his gratitude, gave him gold, silver and twelve pitchers of fragrant wine. In the meantime, however, the inhabitants of the conquered city warned their neighbours, who attacked the Achaeans. After a battle lasting a whole day, Odysseus was forced to set sail, leaving behind more than seventy dead.

The hero then headed south to Maleas, but the seas carried him beyond Cythera. For nine days he was tossed on unknown seas, and on the tenth he made land at the country of the Lotus-eaters, who lived on an exotic flower or fruit, the lotus. Any stranger who arrived in their country and was beguiled into eating the lotus forgot his own homeland. This was the case with three of the Achaeans, but Odysseus, ignoring their lamentations, tied them firmly to the benches of the ships and set sail once more. Continuing on his voyage, without knowing where he was heading, he came upon the island of the Cyclopes.

As soon as he disembarked, the hero chose twelve of his bravest men, took a skin full of Ismarian wine, and set out to explore the island. Soon he came to a cave full of cheese, sheep and goats. In vain did his companions urge him that they should take what they could and make a quick getaway. Odysseus insisted on staying to meet the owner of the cave. So at twilight they saw the huge Cyclops Polyphemus, son of Poseidon and Thoosa, daughter of Phorcys, returning to his cave. Ignoring the words of Odysseus, who called upon him to respect the laws of hospitality, the Cyclops snatched up

Maron, priest of Apollo in the land of the Cicones, gives Odysseus a skin full of sweet wine. Next to the two men stand Opora and Ampelis, personifications of the harvest and the vineyard. (Sicilian krater, mid 4th century BC).

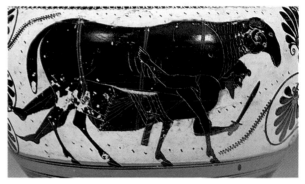

Odysseus, tied underneath the belly of a ram, emerges unknown to the Cyclops, from the cave of Polyphemus. (Black-figure krater, c. 500 BC).

In this vase-painting, three separate episodes from the story of Odysseus and Polyphemus have been amalgamated into a single scene. The hero and his men are blinding the Cyclops, at the same time giving him strong wine to get him drunk; he has not yet finished off their companion. (Laconian kylix, c. 550 BC).

two of Odysseus's men and ate them. The next morning, Polyphemus left, having first blocked the entrance to the cave with an enormous rock. Odysseus saw that he would have to resort to trickery.

That evening, the hero approached Polyphemus, who had devoured two more of his companions, and offered him some wine. Pleased with this, the Cyclops asked him his name, and Odysseus replied that he was called 'Nobody'.

The Cyclopes

The Cyclopes, a savage and uncivilised people, with only one eye in the middle of their forehead, had no other occupation but that of shepherds. It had not occurred to them to organise cities to live in. Each lived with his wives and children in caves on the mountain tops, without being greatly interested in relations with his neighbours.

He then continued to pour wine for Polyphemus until the Cyclops was drunk and fell into a deep sleep. Losing no time, the hero took up a branch of olive, which he had already sharpened at one end, heated it in the fire, and with the help of four of his companions, thrust it deep into the Cyclops' single eye. He, maddened by pain, began to call for help, but when the other Cyclopes arrived and asked him what the matter was, he replied that Nobody had blinded him, so they went away again without taking any notice. When dawn came, Polyphemus stood at the entrance to the cave and felt the backs of the rams which were going out to graze, ready to grab any of the men who tried to slip out together with the flock. But the Achaeans were too clever for him. They tied themselves under the bellies of the animals and succeeded in escaping in that way. As their ships were sailing away, the hero called out: 'If anyone asks you, Cyclops, who took out your eye, tell them that it was Odysseus, son of Laertes, from Ithaca'. Enraged, Polyphemus raised his hands towards heaven and called upon his father, Poseidon, to punish Odysseus. And the god heard his prayer.

165

Circe stirs the magical drink with her staff, preparing to offer it to Odysseus. One of the transformed Achaeans departs, looking uneasily behind him. (Black-figure lekythos with white background, 490 - 480 BC).

From the island of **Aeolus** to the island of **Circe**

*L*eaving the land of the Cyclopes, the fleet of Odysseus anchored at Aeolia, a floating island ringed with walls of bronze where Aeolus, lord of the winds, lived with his wife and children. For a whole month Aeolus entertained Odysseus and his men. Then he shut all the winds, except Zephyrus, the west wind, in a large bag, which he gave to the hero, with instructions not to open it during

One of the companions of Odysseus opens the bag of Aeolus. The head of some wind god, who has already begun to blow menacingly, can be seen emerging from the opening. (Etruscan seal-stone, second half of 5th century BC).

his voyage, and sent him on his way. Carried along by Zephyrus, the ships of Odysseus sailed along for nine days and nine nights, but when they came close to the shores of Ithaca, the hero, conquered by weariness, fell asleep, and his companions, thinking that the bag which Aeolus had given him contained silver and gold, opened it. A tremendous storm immediately broke out, and the fleet of Odysseus was driven back to the island of Aeolus, who, however, refused to help the hero a second time.

Seven days later, Odysseus set eyes on the land of the Laestrygonians. He sent two of his companions, together with a herald, to discover who lived in those parts. They were in for a very unpleasant surprise: the inhabitants of the country were savage giants and their king, Antiphates, devoured one of the Achaeans, while the other two took to their heels. Immediately the Laestrygonians ran down to the shore and began to hurl enormous rocks, crushing the ships of the Achaeans and killing their crews. Odysseus's ship, which was tied up outside the harbour, alone survived this disaster, together with the forty-five men who were travelling in it.

The next stop on their voyage was Aeaea, the island of the goddess Circe, the

The gigantic Laestrygonians, armed with rocks and stones, attack the Greek ships. (Wall-painting from a house on the Esquiline Hill in Rome, c. mid 1st century BC).

Circe, in the middle of the picture, holds the instruments of her magic. Around her, the Achaeans, transformed into a lion, boars, a ram, and a wolf, make gestures of despair and supplication. Eurylochus runs in fear to the right, while Odysseus arrives from the left, determined to save his men. (Black-figure kylix, c. 550 BC).

The Winds

The Winds, Boreas (the North Wind), Zephyrus (the West Wind), and Notus (the South Wind) were also gods, children of Eos and Astraeus, son of the Titan Creius and Eurybia. Some add another wind, Eurus, the personification of the South-east Wind.

The country of the Laestrygonians

Homer tells us that in the country of the Laestrygonians a shepherd who is returning with his flocking from grazing is greeted by another who at the same time is just taking out his own flock - so close are the roads of day and night. From ancient times to the present this puzzling statement has defied explanation. Most scholars supposed that some echo of the information that in the countries of the extreme north the nights are very short in summer lies behind it.

daughter of the Sun. Here the investigation of the place was undertaken by half of the men of the crew, led by Eurylochus. Circe gave a friendly welcome to the Achaeans, but as soon as they entered her palace she gave them a drink which had magic herbs mixed into it which had the power to make them forget their homeland. When they had drunk this, she touched them with her rod and changed them into swine. In vain did Eurylochus, the only one who had not been taken in by the apparent cordiality of the goddess, wait for them outside the palace. When he realised that some new disaster had overtaken them, he hastened off to tell Odysseus. The hero then set out to deal with the witch on his own. As his luck would have it, Hermes appeared at that moment and gave him a herb - 'moly' - to protect him from witchcraft. So the spells of Circe failed and the goddess invited Odysseus to share her bed, having first turned his companions back into men - and indeed younger and more handsome than they had been before. After a year of living at ease in the palace of Circe, the Achaeans resolved that the time had come to set out for home. But when Odysseus told Circe of their departure, she advised him to visit Hades first, to learn from the soul of the seer Tiresias how he could reach Ithaca at last.

167

Odysseus in Hades

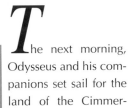

*T*he next morning, Odysseus and his companions set sail for the land of the Cimmer-

Odysseus, sitting before the gates of Hades, holds his sword in his hand to drive away the souls who approach to drink blood. He looks, with a distant gaze, at Elpenor, who appears from the chasm. Behind the hero is Hermes, whose presence is not mentioned by Homer, but is explained by the fact that it was he who led the dead to Acheron to deliver them to Charon. (Red-figure pelike, c. 440 BC).

ians, which was at the furthest bounds of Oceanus and which was covered with total darkness. Following the instructions of Circe, the hero advanced alongside the stream of Oceanus, the great river which, the Greeks believed, ringed the earth, until he came to the entrance to Hades. There, when he had dug a pit and poured libations to the dead, he slaughtered a black ram and a black ewe. Soon the spirits of the dead began to gather round the pit, thirsting to drink blood, but Odysseus kept them at bay, waiting for Tiresias to arrive first. At that moment, Elpenor, one of his companions who had fallen from the roof of Circe's house on the day of their departure and had been killed without their realising it, made his appearance. As he was still unburied, Elpenor spoke without having first to drink blood and asked Odysseus to arrange for his burial. Then Tiresias arrived, drank blood, and revealed to the hero that Poseidon was angry with him because of the blinding of Polyphemus and would do everything in his power to hinder their return home. However, Odysseus and his companions would be able to return to Ithaca, the seer continued, as long as they did not harm the cattle of the Sun when they put in at Thrinacia. If, on the other hand, they slaughtered any of the god's animals, Odysseus would reach his native island only after innumerable hardships, alone and in the vessel of another. And there new troubles would await him, since many arrogant princelings had gathered in his palace, seeking to marry his wife, Penelope.

As soon as Tiresias had departed, Odysseus allowed other souls to drink blood so that

Odysseus, sitting before the gates of Hades between Eurylochus and Perimedes, listens carefully to the advice and oracles of the blind seer Tiresias, whose head can be seen near the feet of the hero. (Lucanian krater, 400 - 390 BC).

they could speak. First his mother, Anticlea, presented herself and told him that Penelope had remained faithful to him and that his father, Laertes, had withdrawn to his estate in the countryside, where he lived a life embittered by the disappearance of his only son. Next to appear was a series of many women from the previous generation of women who told their own stories. These were followed by the soul of Agamemnon, who told Odysseus of his tragic murder. Last to come was Achilles, accompanied by his friends Patroclus, Antilochus and Ajax, son of Telamon. Achilles heard with satisfaction from the mouth of Odysseus of the feats of his son Neoptolemos, but Ajax stood some way off, still angry over the matter of the weapons of Achilles. Odysseus also saw Minos giving judgment with a golden rod in his hand, Sisyphus and Tantalus being eternally punished, and Achilles - but only his shade, because the hero himself was on Olympus together with the other gods. Then, as he was surrounded by innumerable souls of the dead wanting to drink blood, he took fright and ran off to join his companions. Without loss of time, they all jumped into their ship and, thanks to a favourable wind, were soon back on the island of Circe.

Danaus and the Danaids

Danaus, son of the King of Egypt, Belus, quarrelled with his brother Aegyptus after the death of their father, either over the sharing out of their inheritance, or because Danaus, who had fifty daughters, envied Aegyptus, who had fifty sons. Danaus took his daughters and fled to Argos, where he became king. Later, Aegyptus sent his sons to Argos to marry the daughters of Danaus. But they, on their father's instructions, all - with the exception of one or two - killed their husbands on the first night of their marriage. For this reason, in Hades, the Danaids were condemned to struggle eternally to fill a vessel full of holes - the 'jar of the Danaids' - with water.

169

From the Sirens toThrinacia

Bound to a column, which represents the mast of his ship, Odysseus listens to the sweet sound of the pipe which a Siren is playing. Next to him, a dolphin leaps out of the water. (Black-figure lekythos with off-white background, c. 500 BC).

*O*dysseus did not stay long on Aeaea. When he had buried Elpenor and listened to the instructions of Circe about the voyage, he bade her farewell and set out once more for his homeland. The first island which he encountered was that of the Sirens, demonic beings who led astray seamen with their song. Following the advice of Circe, Odysseus plugged the ears of his crew with wax so that they were unable to hear the Sirens. He himself, however, did not wish to miss the song, and so he ordered his men to tie him to the mast and not to release him however much he begged them. As they drew close to the island, Odysseus heard the Sirens calling him by name and inviting him to stay with them. Immediately, his mind became confused: he forgot the glories of the past, his homeland and his wife, and the only thing he longed for was to go ashore to enjoy the entrancing song without interruption. But he signalled to no avail to his companions to set him free; they simply bound him tighter, in accordance with his instructions. When they had passed by the island of the Sirens, the seamen, relieved that they had escaped the danger, unblocked their ears and released their leader.

In order to continue on his way, Odysseus had to choose between two routes. The first led to the Wandering Rocks, those notorious cliffs which only the famous Argo had succeeded in escaping, while the second was through the straits of Scylla and Charybdis. Circe's opinion had been that they should avoid the Wandering Rocks and the rock of Charybdis, which would mean certain disaster for all of them, and to choose to pass close to the rock of Scylla. It was this latter route that Odysseus decided to follow, in the hope that he would manage to get away without losing any of his men. But at the mo-

According to one tradition, the Sirens, when they failed to allure Odysseus with their song, threw themselves into the sea and committed suicide. This seems to be the subject of this scene, which shows a Siren falling headlong from a rock, with her eyes closed, while another, on the left, opens her wings to follow her sister to her death. (Red-figure stamnos, c. 475 BC).

Scylla and Charybdis

Scylla, a terrible monster with twelve legs, six heads and a voice like the barking of a pup, had her nest on a rock in the sea whose top reached to the sky. It was from up there that she stretched out her long necks as far as the surface of the sea to snatch up some large fish or sailors from passing vessels. Opposite Scylla, from a lower rock, lived Charybdis. Lurking beneath a wild fig tree, this monster sucked in the water of the sea three times a day and three times a day regurgitated it. If, of course, any ship happen to be close at hand, it would be sunk with all hands.

The belief of seamen in the existence of monsters which haunted the seas finds expression on this coin in the enormous crab and the demonic Scylla, who shades her eyes with her hand to look out for fresh victims on the horizon. (Silver four-drachma coin of Acragas, 420 - 415 BC).

ment when they were passing between the two rocks, Charybdis sucked in the water, making the seamen's blood run cold with fear. This was the moment which Scylla had been waiting for. Pouncing upon them, she ate six of the bravest of the Achaeans before the eyes of their companions.

After this dramatic encounter with Scylla, the Achaeans, rowing hard, reached the island of Thrinacia, where the cattle of the Sun grazed. Odysseus, remembering the words of Tiresias, did not want to stop. But when his companions swore that they would not touch the animals, he agreed that they should go ashore. As their ill fortune would have it, the next morning a tremendous storm broke and kept them marooned on the island for a whole month. As long as the provisions which Circe had given them lasted, the Achaeans did not violate their oath, but when these came to an end, taking advantage of the absence of Odysseus, who had withdrawn to pray to the gods, they satisfied their hunger by slaughtering the fattest of the god's cattle. Seven days later, the wind dropped and the Achaeans hurriedly put to sea. But as soon as they had left Thrinacia behind, Zeus, who had promised the Sun that he would punish those responsible for the slaughter of his cattle, split their ship in two with a thunderbolt.

171

From the island of Calypso t the island of the Phaeacians

Odysseus, holding the branch of a suppliant, approaches the daughters of the Phaeacians. Next to him, Athena looks at him protectively. (Red-figure amphora, 450 - 440 BC).

*T*he only one to escape alive from the shipwreck caused by Zeus was Odysseus, who had refused to taste the flesh of the Sun's cattle. Hanging on to the mast and hull of his ship, which he had bound together with a rope, he was carried by the wind to the rock of Charybdis, at the time when the monster was sucking in the water. But at the moment when the hull and the mast were sinking into the abyss, the hero leapt up high and siezed hold of the wild fig tree which grew above the home of Chraybdis. He remained hanging there for many hours, until he saw the remains of his ship resurfacing in the foam. He jumped on to them and began to row with his hands in order to escape from there as quickly as he could. After wrestling with the waves for nine days and nights, the gods threw him upon the shore of Ogygia, the island of the beautiful nymph Calypso.

The immortal Calyso, daughter of Atlas, received the castaway with love, and lost no time in uniting herself with him. To begin with, the enchanting beauty of Ogygia and the kindness of the nymph charmed Odysseus, but soon he began to experience an unbearable longing for his home. In spite of this, the hero was forced to stay for seven whole years with Calypso, who had in the meantime fallen in love with him. In the end, one morning when Poseidon, his great enemy, had left Olympus to visit the country of the Ethiopians, Zeus, egged on by Athena and with the agreement of the other gods, sent Hermes to the nymph to tell her to let Odysseus go. She, though the parting cost her dearly, had to obey the will of the gods. So she helped her beloved to construct a raft, gave him instructions for his journey, and said goodbye to him for ever.

For seventeen days and nights Odysseus floated on the raft, until Poseidon, returning

On the day on which Odysseus came ashore on Scheria, Nausicaa, prompted by Athena, went with the girls of her entourage to the sea-shore to wash clothes. Here Odysseus emerges hesitantly from behind the bushes, trying to cover his nakedness, in order to approach the princess. In front of him, Athena urges him to follow her. Two girls, Philonoe and Leucippe, run away startled by the sudden appearance of the hero. Another, Cleopatra, continues to be absorbed in the washing. Nausicaa alone, emboldened by the secret intervention of the goddess, remains unperturbed, but thoughtful, waiting to hear the stranger's story. (Lid of a red-figure pyxis, 450 - 425 BC).

Penelope

Penelope was a daughter of Icarius, brother of Tyndareus, and of the Naiad Periboea. According to tradition, her father arranged races and offered his daughter as a prize for the victor. The races were won by Odysseus, who thus was counted worthy to become the husband of the beautiful and intelligent Penelope.

from the country of the Ethiopians, caught sight of him and, raising a huge wave, hurled him into the turbulent sea. But thanks to the sea goddess Leucothea, the hero survived, and, three days later, was washed ashore exhausted on the coast of Scheria, where the people of the Phaeacians lived. There he met Nausicaa, daughter of King Alcinous, who saw to it that he had clothing and food and advised him to present himself at the palace and fall at the knees of her mother, imploring her to help him, which he did. Alcinous, favourable impressed by the appearance and wise words of the stranger, promised him that he would equip one of the famous ships of the Phaeacians and send him off the very next day to his home. He also held a splendid banquet to honour his guest. In the course of the celebrations, the blind bard Demodocus sang of an episode from the Trojan War, and Odysseus, unable to contain himself, burst into tears. Only Alcinous noticed the hero's emotion, but, discreetly, said nothing. Later, however, when Odysseus, at the farewell meal, again wept on hearing Demodocus sing the story of the Trojan Horse, Alcinous stopped the bard and asked his guest to reveal his identity. To their amazement, the Phaeacians learnt that their guest was none other than the renowned Odysseus. Later, the hero, in order to express his thanks, told them of his adventures in every detail. The next day, the Phaeacians loaded Odysseus with rich gifts and provided him with a ship, which, quick as lightning, brought him to Ithaca.

In this scene Odysseus is shown leaving the cave of Charybdis, not hanging on to the remains of his ship as tradition narrates, but on a huge sea turtle. (Black-figure skyphos, early 5th century BC).

173

Odysseus on Ithaca

Oddyseus, as a humble beggar, takes the hand of the sorrowful Penelope. Behind her, Telemachus (?) and two old men, Laertes (?), standing, and the swineherd Eumaeus (?), sitting on the ground, watch the scene. ('Melian' relief, c. 460 - 450 BC).

*O*n Ithaca, where people had long ceased to believe that Odysseus would return, the palace was full of young men from noble families who were pressing Penelope to be their wife. She, in order to buy time, said that she would select her second husband as soon as she had woven a shroud for old Laetres. The suitors agreed, but the shroud never seemed to be going to be finished. This was because what Penelope wove by day, she unravelled at night. In this way three years passed, until a slave-girl told the suitors of her mistress's trickery. They, in order to blackmail her into making up her mind, gathered every morning in the palace of Odysseus, eating, drinking and merrymaking, and thus wasting his fortune.

This was the situation when the Phaeacians left Odysseus, who during the voyage had fallen into a deep sleep, on a shore of Ithaca. As soon as the hero awoke, he was transformed into a beggar by Athena so that no one should recognise him, and set off to find his faithful swineherd Eumaeus. In a little while his only son, Telemachus, arrived there too, having just returned from a journey to Pylos and Sparta, where he had hoped to hear news of his father's fate. Odysseus made himself known to his son at once, and together they laid a plan to punish the suitors. When, still disguised as a beggar, he reached his palace, the hero saw, with tears in his eyes, his beloved dog Argus, now very old, who recognised him, wagged his tail in joy, and soon afterwards died.

As was to be expected, the suitors behaved cruelly and offensively towards the unknown beggar. Oddyseus, however, found the opportunity to approach Penelope and to assure her that her husband was alive. Deeply moved, Penelope ordered her maidservants to look after the stranger. Euryclea, his old nurse, realised who he was when, as she washed his feet, she came upon a scar from some old hunting injury. But Odysseus ordered her not to reveal to anyone that he had returned.

Odysseus draws his bow against the suitors, while behind him two slave-girls look on anxiously. (Red-figure skyphos, c. 450 BC).

The suitors, taken by surprise and panic-stricken, snatch up whatever comes to hand to protect themselves from the arrows of Odysseus. One of them has already been wounded. (Red-figure skyphos, c. 450 BC).

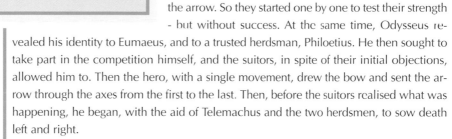

The end of Odysseus

According to the prophecy of Tiresias, death would come to Odysseus *'ex halos'* - 'out of the sea' or 'from the sea'. In fact it turned out that the latter was the correct interpretation of the oracle. Telegonus, son of Circe and Odysseus, who had set out to find his father, put in on the coast of Ithaca and, without knowing where he was, slaughtered some animals. Odysseus hastened to deal with the invader, and in the battle which ensued, Telegonus killed the hero with a spear which had at its tip, instead of sharpened metal, the poisonous sting of a huge sting-ray.

Penelope sits in distress before the loom with the half-finished shroud of old Laertes. The young man with his proud bearing who stands in front of her, looking at her thoughtfully, is her son Telemachus. (Red-figure skyphos, c. 440 BC).

The next day, Penelope announced to the suitors that she would marry whoever managed to draw the bow of Odysseus and pierce twelve axes placed in a row with the arrow. So they started one by one to test their strength - but without success. At the same time, Odysseus revealed his identity to Eumaeus, and to a trusted herdsman, Philoetius. He then sought to take part in the competition himself, and the suitors, in spite of their initial objections, allowed him to. Then the hero, with a single movement, drew the bow and sent the arrow through the axes from the first to the last. Then, before the suitors realised what was happening, he began, with the aid of Telemachus and the two herdsmen, to sow death left and right.

When Penelope learnt, from the faithful Euryclea, that her husband had returned, she refused to believe it. Although Odysseus had now taken on his real form, he seemed a stranger to her. But a secret which was known only to the two of them convinced her that the miracle had happened. In her happiness, she threw herself into the hero's arms, and then they shut themselves in their room to enjoy their love. And the night went on and on, because Athena did not permit Eos, the goddess of dawn, to make her appearance.

The next day Odysseus went to show himself to his father, Laertes, who lived all alone in the countryside, and took him back with him to the palace. In the meantime, the relatives of the dead suitors had resolved to take revenge, but, fortunately, thanks to the intervention of Athena, conflict was avoided. The trials of Odysseus, the most sorely-tried of the heroes of the Trojan War, were now at an end.

Index

Sources of illustration

Ekdotike Athenon would like to thank the museums, collections, academic institutions and photographic agencies which have assisted in the illustration of this book.

Abbreviations: t = top, c = centre, b = bottom, l = left, r = right. The numbers refer to the pages.

6t Berlin, Staatliche Museen - Antikensammlung.
6c New York, Metropolitan Museum of Art.
7 Athens, National Archaeological Museum.
10 Berlin, Staatliche Museen - Antikensammlung.
11t Berlin, Staatliche Museen - Antikensammlung, Pergamonmuseum.
11b London, British Museum.
12t New York, Metropolitan Museum of Art.
12c Paris, Musie du Louvre.
13 Rome, Museo Capitolino.
14 Athens, National Archaeological Museum.
15t Corfu, Archaeological Museum.
15b Naples, Museo Archeologico Nazionale (Phot. Scala).
16t Berlin, Staatliche Museen - Antikensammlung, Pergamonmuseum.
16b Berlin, Staatliche Museen - Antikensammlung.
17t Berlin, Staatliche Museen - Antikensammlung, Pergamonmuseum. 17cl Ferrara, Museo Archeologico Nazionale di Spina.
17cr Naples, Museo Archeologico Nazionale.
18 Cerveteri, Museo Nazionale Cerite.
19 Munich, Staatliche Antikensammlungen.
20 Oxford, Ashmolean Museum.
21 Rome, Museo Capitolino.
22t Rome, Museo Capitolino.
22b Vatican, Musei Vaticani.
23t Oxford, Ashmolean Museum.
23c Paris, Bibliothnque Nationale.
26c Berlin, Staatliche Museen - Antikensammlung.
26b Berlin, Staatliche Museen - Antikensammlung.
27tl Munich, Staatliche Antikensammlungen und Glyptothek.
27tr Munich, Staatliche Antikensammlungen.
27b London, British Museum.
28 Malibu, Cal., J. Paul Getty Museum.
29t Paris, Bibliothnque Nationale.
29b Ferrara, Museo Archeologico Nazionale di Spina.
30t Berlin, Staatliche Museen - Antikensammlung.
30b Munich, Staatliche Antikensammlungen.
31 Naples, Museo Archeologico Nazionale.
32t Athens, Acropolis Museum.
32b Piraeus, Archaeological Museum.

33t Basel, Antikenmuseum und Sammlung Ludwig.
33b Athens, National Archaeological Museum.
34t Vienna, Kunsthistorisches Museum.
34b Athens, National Archaeological Museum.
35tl Munich, Antikensammlungen und Glyptothek.
35tr Paris, Bibliothnque Nationale.
35c Pella, Archaeological Museum.
36 Berlin, Staatliche Museen - Antikensammlung, Pergamonmuseum.
37tl Athens, National Archaeological Museum.
37tr London, British Museum.
37c London, British Museum.
38t Athens, National Archaeological Museum.
38c Olympia, Archaeological Museum.
39t London, British Museum.
39b Vatican, Musei Vaticani.
40t London, British Museum.
40c Boston, Museum of Fine Arts.
40b Kassel, Staatliche Kunstsammlungen.
41 Munich, Staatliche Antikensammlungen.
42 St Petersburg, Hermitage Museum.
43t Florence, Museo Archeologico.
43b Boston, Museum of Fine Arts.
44t Paris, Musie du Louvre.
44c Olympia, Archaeological Museum.
45t Athens, National Archaeological Museum.
45c Berlin, Staatliche Museen - Antikensammlung.
45b Boston, Museum of Fine Arts.
46c Rome, Museo Nazionale Romano (Phot. Scala).
46b Tarquinia, Museo Nazionale Tarquiniense.
47t Naples, Museo Archeologico Nazionale.
47c Florence, Museo Archeologico.
48 Paris, Musie du Louvre.
49t Rome, Museo Nazionale Romano (Phot. Scala).
49cl London, British Museum.
49cr Athens, National Archaeological Museum.
50 Munich, Staatliche Antikensammlungen.
51t Berlin, Staatliche Museen - Antikensammlung.
51c Berlin, Staatliche Museen - Antikensammlung.
52t Thessaloniki, Archaeological Museum.
52b Paris, Bibliothnque Nationale.
53t Delos.
53c Naples, Museo Archeologico Nazionale (Phot. Pedicini).

53b Athens, National Archaeological Museum.
54 Athens, National Archaeological Museum.
55 Athens, National Archaeological Museum.
56 Reggio di Calabria, Museo Archeologico Nazionale.
57t Athens, National Archaeological Museum.
57c London, British Museum.
58t Berlin, Staatliche Museen - Antikensammlung, Pergamonmuseum.
58b Tarquinia, Museo Nazionale Tarquiniense.
59tl Munich, Staatliche Antikensammlungen.
59tr Munich, Staatliche Antikensammlungen.
59c Venice, Museo Archeologico.
60 Munich, Staatliche Antikensammlungen.
61 Paris, Bibliothnque Nationale.
62 Eretria, Archaeological Museum.
63 Munich, Staatliche Antikensammlungen und Glyptothek.
64 Würzburg, Martin von Wagner Museum.
65t London, British Museum.
65b London, British Museum.
66 Paris, Musie du Louvre.
67 Munich, Staatliche Antikensammlungen.
68 Madrid, Museo Arqueologico Nacional.
70 Brescia, Museo Romano.
71t Palermo, Museo Archeologico Regionale.
71c Basel, Antikenmuseum und Sammlung Ludwig.
71b Paris, Musie du Louvre.
72 London, British Museum.
73 Paris, Musie du Louvre.
74c Olympia, Archaeological Museum.
74b London, British Museum.
75t Palermo, Museo Archeologico Regionale.
75b Naples, Museo Archeologico Nazionale.
76 Olympia, Archaeological Museum.
77t Paris, Musie du Louvre.
77c Munich, Staatliche Antikensammlungen.
77b London, British Museum.
78 Paris, Musie du Louvre.
79t Taranto, Museo Archeologico Nazionale.
79c Berlin, Staatliche Museen - Antikensammlung.
79b Athens, National Archaeological Museum.
80 Athens, National Archaeological Museum.
81 Munich, Staatliche Antikensammlungen.

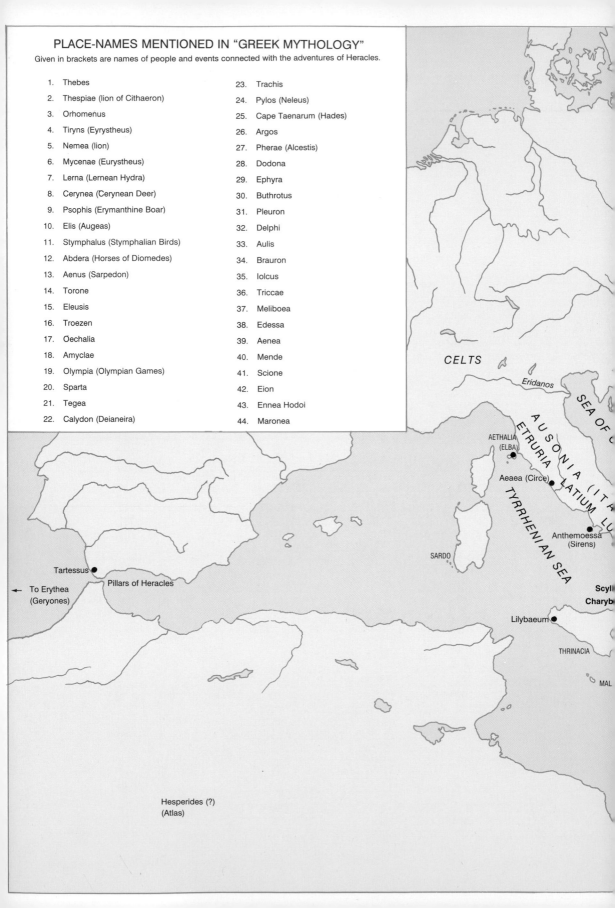

PLACE-NAMES MENTIONED IN "GREEK MYTHOLOGY"

Given in brackets are names of people and events connected with the adventures of Heracles.

1. Thebes
2. Thespiae (lion of Cithaeron)
3. Orhomenus
4. Tiryns (Eyrystheus)
5. Nemea (lion)
6. Mycenae (Eurystheus)
7. Lerna (Lernean Hydra)
8. Cerynea (Cerynean Deer)
9. Psophis (Erymanthine Boar)
10. Elis (Augeas)
11. Stymphalus (Stymphalian Birds)
12. Abdera (Horses of Diomedes)
13. Aenus (Sarpedon)
14. Torone
15. Eleusis
16. Troezen
17. Oechalia
18. Amyclae
19. Olympia (Olympian Games)
20. Sparta
21. Tegea
22. Calydon (Deianeira)
23. Trachis
24. Pylos (Neleus)
25. Cape Taenarum (Hades)
26. Argos
27. Pherae (Alcestis)
28. Dodona
29. Ephyra
30. Buthrotus
31. Pleuron
32. Delphi
33. Aulis
34. Brauron
35. Iolcus
36. Triccae
37. Meliboea
38. Edessa
39. Aenea
40. Mende
41. Scione
42. Eion
43. Ennea Hodoi
44. Maronea

CELTS

Eridanos

SEA OF

AETHALIA
(ELBA)

AUSONIA (ITA
ETRURIA LATIUM LU

Aeaea (Circe)

TYRRHENIAN SEA

Anthemoessa
(Sirens)

SARDO

Tartessus

Pillars of Heracles

← To Erythea
(Geryones)

Scyl
Charyb

Lilybaeum

THRINACIA

MAL

Hesperides (?)
(Atlas)

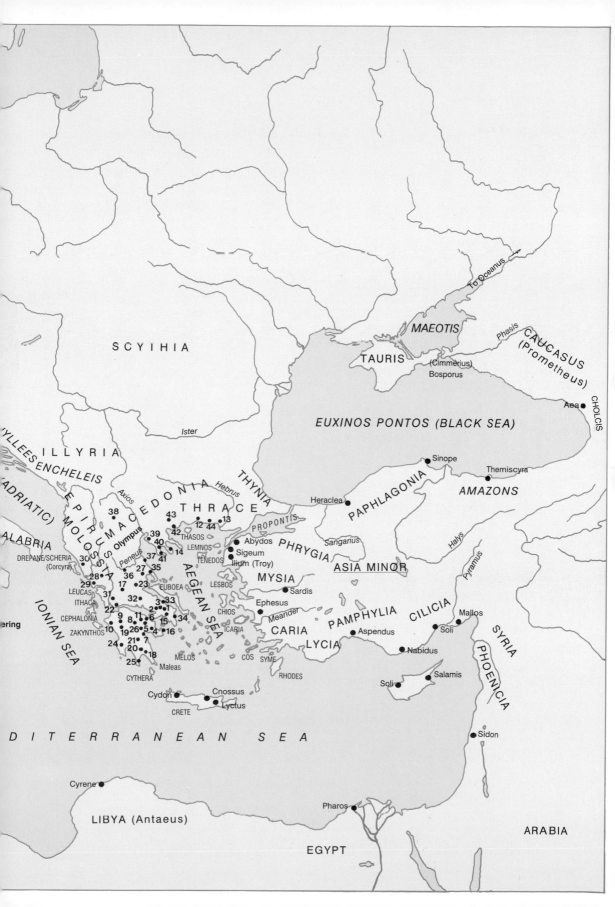

SCYIHIA

ILLYRIA

(KYLLEES) ENCHELEIS

(ADRIATIC)

CALABRIA

DREPANE/SCHERIA
(Corcyra)

MOLOSSIA

EPIRUS

MACEDONIA

Axios

Olympus

Peneus

LEUCAS

ITHACA

CEPHALONIA

ZAKYNTHOS

IONIAN SEA

ering

THRACE

Hebrus

THASOS

LEMNOS

TENEDOS

EUBOEA

AEGEAN SEA

LESBOS

CHIOS

ICARIA

MELOS

COS

CYTHERA

Maleas

SYME

RHODES

Cydon

Cnossus

CRETE

Lyctus

THYNIA

PROPONTIS

Abydos

Sigeum

Ilium (Troy)

PHRYGIA

Sangarius

ASIA MINOR

MYSIA

Sardis

Ephesus

Meander

CARIA

LYCIA

PAMPHYLIA

Aspendus

Nabidus

CILICIA

Soli

Mallos

Pyramus

Halys

Heraclea

PAPHLAGONIA

Sinope

AMAZONS

Themiscyra

MAEOTIS

TAURIS

(Cimmerius)
Bosporus

EUXINOS PONTOS (BLACK SEA)

Phasis

CAUCASUS
(Prometheus)

Aea

CHOLCIS

Ister

SYRIA

PHOENICIA

Soli

Salamis

Sidon

MEDITERRANEAN SEA

Cyrene

LIBYA (Antaeus)

EGYPT

Pharos

ARABIA

38
43
12 44 13
42
39 40 14
37 41
27 35
30
17 23
28
29
31
32
22 9
11 6
8 5
10 26 4 16
19 7
24 21 20
25 18
3 33
2 1
15 34